INTERNATIONALLY KNOWN

SEQUEL TO NEW YORK'S

KS Publications
www.kikiswinson.net

Publisher's address:

K.S. Publications
P.O. Box 68878
Virginia Beach, VA 23471

Website: www.kikiswinson.net
Email: KS.publications@yahoo.com

ISBN-13: 978-0984529018
ISBN-10: 0984529012

First Edition: November 2012

10 9 8 7 6 5 4 3 2

Editors: John Wooden & Letitia Carrington
Interior & Cover Design: Davida Baldwin (OddBalldsgn.com)
Cover Photo: Davida Baldwin

Printed in the United States of America

Don't Miss Out On These Other Titles:

PRELUDE

I had to get myself together mentally after that incident at the airport. It had become a daunting task just to calm my nerves after I took the wig off my head. It seemed like the harder I tried to be optimistic about surviving this thing; a gut wrenching thought of me wearing prison orange kept dancing in my head. The thought of prison life wasn't something I looked forward to. In addition to being arrested, I also thought about how Miguel was going to react when he found out about his shipment. I was sure it would be confiscated once a thorough investigation was completed. I needed to figure out how to rectify this situation.

On our way to the city, I had questions for Evan. I needed some answers. "How did you know where I was? And why did you come for me?" I asked him.

"The airport is tight with security and no one is allowed down in my area of the loading dock but my crew, and when I saw a lot of unfamiliar faces show up in the loading area, I knew something was about to go down. So I called my men off the site and sent them to another gate area until I found out what was going on. And when I started asking questions and couldn't get any answers about why they were setting up surveillance in my loading port, I knew your shipment was their target, so I switched gears and got out of there."

"Well, how did you know where I was?" I repeated the question.

KIKI SWINSON

"I watched you from the time you got off the plane."

"So, why did you save me from them? I mean if I were you I would've been trying to save myself."

"Naomi, it's gonna come out that me and my men were going to allow that shipment to come in. And when it does, my whole career and retirement is going down the drain. I may be even looking to do some serious time too, so I figured I needed an insurance policy."

Baffled by Evan's words, I tried to define his words in layman's terms. I wanted to know what the fuck he was talking about when he said he needed *an insurance policy*. Then all of a sudden it clicked. He wanted some money from me. A dollar amount hadn't been uttered from his lips, but I knew it was coming next.

I looked back at Evan who happened to be a very small man in stature, but I remembered he mentioned to me some time ago that he worked out at least four days a week. When I took a good look at his upper body, I saw the muscles around his shoulders as clear as day. This Puerto Rican cat would probably beat my black ass in the back of an alley real bad if I didn't give him what he wanted. He had been an associate of mines for a long time and he had been loyal to me, so I guess he figured it was time for him to cash out and go off on his own. Clearly, it was every man for himself.

Pretending to stay calm, I said, "What kind of an insurance policy are we talking about?"

"For where I am going, I am going to need five hundred thousand dollars," he said without blinking an eye. Nor did his expression change. This guy acted like he was dead serious.

I thought for a moment about how much money I had back at my place. I knew that it wasn't near the amount he asked for, but I hoped that it would help buy me some time. "Evan, I don't have five hundred grand at my disposal. But I can get my hands on at least one hundred and fifty."

Evan slammed his fist on the steering wheel. "No!" he roared. "That's not enough. I want five hundred thousand dollars right now. Now if you can't get it to me, then you and I are going to go on a very long ride Chica."

After I watched Evan snap like he'd just done, I got a whole new sense of reality. This guy wasn't stable at all and I hadn't the slightest clue as to what to do next.

"You better think of something real quick because I'm trying to be out of town in the next couple of hours," he concluded.

"Can I make a phone call?" I asked.

"Hell, no! I'm not stupid. You'll try to get me ambushed."

"So, how do you expect me to get the rest of the money for you?"

"Get it from your bank account. I know you gotta have some of it there."

My heart continued to race and my mind wasn't unscrambling my thoughts. I thought I was about to lose my fucking mind. I figured what in the hell could go wrong next? Then it came to me. I was instructed to wait for Damian at our hideaway spot. Damian insisted that he'd meet me there, so that's where I decided to take Evan. Until this very moment, I liked Evan. He was indeed a soldier for our operation, but don't bite the hand that feeds you. That's a fucking no-no! And when it was all said and done, one of his loved ones would be using his insurance policy.

"I can't go to my bank. That's too risky. Take me to my apartment at 145 West 67th Street. I got a drop off I was supposed to deposit in the bank yesterday. There's more than enough in there for you to get your share and for me to take and leave town with," I said.

"Oh, no way, Chica. I'm getting everything you got. I put my neck on the line for you. You owe me for all those times you underpaid me for helping you to bring in your fucking drugs," he growled. His facial expression got more menacing.

I remained calm. I knew something he didn't, his life was coming to a screeching halt when Damian found out he intended to rob us. Talk about a sad ending.

As we approached the apartment building, I searched both sides of the block to see if I saw Reggie or Damian's cars parked anywhere, but I didn't. The optimism of getting Evan off my back dissipated rapidly. The fear that had left my heart crept right back in at that very moment. I had to fight this battle all by myself. I started to stall him, but I knew that would only piss him off, so I climbed out of the truck and made my way up to the apartment while Evan followed.

I fumbled with the key at the front door so he snatched the keys away from me and unlocked it himself. Immediately after he opened the front door, he pushed me inside but instructed me to stand where he could see me.

Before he made his entrance, he peeped around the door to make sure the coast was clear with his gun cocked and ready to fire. I stood there and faced him head on trying to figure out how I would handle this situation.

"Now, let's get that money," he said, and then he turned his back to shut the front door behind himself. Evan turning his back on me gave me a big enough window to make a run for Reggie's bedroom, so I could grab his moneybag and jump from the window.

But plans don't always go as planned. As soon as I turned to dip in the opposite direction, Reggie came out of nowhere and startled the crap out of me. It all happened so damn fast. After Reggie pressed his hand against my mouth to keep me from screaming, he pushed me off to the side.

As soon as Evan turned around, he realized things had changed. He had never met Reggie, so he never knew what he looked like. I guessed he was about to find out. I wasn't sure, but something told me Evan knew he was face-to-face with the head of our operation. "Look, all I want is what's owed to me," Evan said as he kept close to the front door.

"I don't owe you shit. You came here to rob us," I spat.

"Nigga, you came here to rob me and my sister?" Reggie roared as he pointed his pistol with the silencer attached directly at Evan.

"No, she promised to pay me for the load that came in today. And I'm trying to leave town so I need my money," Evan continued as he looked at Reggie and I. I immediately saw the fear in his eyes. He was very afraid of not leaving here alive. Which was a good possibility.

"What load, nigga? We didn't have a load come in today," Reggie challenged him. I knew he was playing head games with Evan. Reggie wasn't about to admit to having any involvement with Miguel's drug shipment whatsoever. Reggie was the type of cat that wouldn't admit to doing shit, even if you caught him in the act.

"I'm talking about that shipment that Naomi ordered me and my boys to offload from the plane earlier, but we couldn't do it because the Feds came in and intercepted it."

"So that means you couldn't do your job, right?" Reggie pressed on.

"We tried, b . . . bu . . . but we couldn't," Evan barely managed to get the words out.

"That's too bad," Reggie said and without warning he pulled the trigger and shot Evan twice in the face. Evan's body fell back against the door and made a loud thud noise. Blood splattered against the front door and on the walls nearby. I swear I couldn't believe my eyes.

"Why the fuck you bring him here?" Reggie questioned me. I knew he was pissed. But I had no other choice.

"Trust me, I didn't mean to," I said weakly. "He saw me trying to get away from the Feds at the airport and tricked me into believing that he was helping me. But when we got into his truck, he started acting crazy and threatening to do shit to me if I didn't give him five hundred grand. I tried to settle with him by giving him the one hundred and fifty grand at my place, but he wouldn't take it. So what was I supposed to do? Let him kill me."

"Come on and help me move this nigga out of the way. Damian and Stone should be here in a minute," he said. I thought he would've answered my question, but he didn't. I guess he figured I didn't have a choice after all.

We grabbed a box of industrial size trash bags we used to wrap our money in and took it to where Evan's body was. Before we touched him, we slipped on plastic gloves and surgical masks.

"Help me grab his legs first," Reggie instructed me. The bags we had were big enough to put a human who was five-five or shorter inside of it. Since Evan was approximately that height, his body fitted the bag perfectly. I believed we covered his body in at least ten bags. When we were done, we wrapped gray duct tape around his waist and we sealed the top of it with six feet of the same tape. Reggie made sure we contained the rest of Evan's blood and the associated odor that came from a dead corpse.

Immediately afterwards, I struggled to clean all of Evan's blood that soaked into the carpet after he was killed. I used ammonia, bleach and baking soda, and when I realized that those cleaners wouldn't do the trick, I grabbed a pair of utility scissors from the kitchen and cut the entire area of the bloodstained carpet and removed it from the floor. I asked Reggie what did he want me to do with it. He simply said, "Lay it on top of that nigga in the bathtub. I'll get Stone and Damian to take it out when they take him out of here."

"All right," I said.

I cleaned up behind myself and made sure that everything I used to dispose of Evan's body with was thrown into another trash bag, while Reggie was in the other room gathering up his things. I heard him counting his money. Then I heard him fumbling with something in his closet. I didn't bother him. I knew he needed this time to figure out our next step, so I made a detour into my bedroom and gathered up my things as well.

Fifteen minutes later, Damian and Stone finally showed up. Stone was ready to walk back out the door the moment he stepped inside the apartment. He made it blatantly obvious that he was ready to get us out of here. "Come on, let's go," he told us. "I've got my other driver outside waiting for us."

But instead of leaving immediately, Reggie decided to run down what happened before Stone and Damian arrived.

INTERNATIONALLY KNOWN

"You know I'll die for you Reggie," Stone retorted quickly. "But it would be a dumb move to move that body while it's still daylight. We're gonna have to change plans."

"Nah, we can't do that. It's gonna fuck up everything," Reggie argued.

Stone wouldn't back down. He was adamant about handling his business a certain way. "I'm sorry. But I won't do it," he told Reggie.

Reggie wasn't used to hearing someone telling him no. He was the boss and he always had the last say in any situation. "Look, Stone, you know I don't like changing plans. That motherfucker came to us with his bullshit. So, we had to deal with it accordingly. And if we hadn't and allowed him to go free, then the cops would've been all over us right now."

Damian and I sat across from each other and waited to see how this thing with Stone and Reggie would play out. We knew we needed to get out of there, but we also knew that we couldn't leave until the body was gone first.

"Why don't y'all leave now and I'll catch up to you later on tonight," Stone suggested.

"But we're gonna need you to drive," Reggie replied. "That was the plan. Remember?"

"Yeah, that was the plan until I found out you had a dead body lying back there in the fucking bathtub."

Damian saw that this ordeal with Reggie and Stone wouldn't be resolved as quickly as we'd liked, so he stood up and said, "Why don't we all stay here until nightfall and then we make a run for it?"

"Nah, that's a dumbass plan," Reggie said crassly. "Our faces will be plastered all over the fucking TV by then. The neighbors in this building know how we look, so believe me when I tell you that they'll blow the whistle on us for some fucking reward money if the Feds say they're offering it."

"He's got a point Damian," I said.

"But what other choice do you have?" Stone chimed in.

"I say we blow this joint now. I got a duffle bag filled with dough that'll last me for a while. And all I need for you to do is get me across the Mexico Border so I can lay low for a few months until this shit blows over. By that time, Vanessa will have let her guard down and brought her stinky ass out of hiding and then boom, I could come back into the states without anyone knowing and have that bitch carved up like a pig on a silver platter."

"And what do we do in the meantime?" I spoke up. I realized that none of Reggie's plans included Damian or me.

"Right now, sis, we have to go our separate ways. It wouldn't be a good look to have all of us going to the same place. We can meet up sometime later though."

"You can go with me out west if you like," Damian suggested. I knew what he was doing, so I played along.

"Are you sure?" I asked.

INTERNATIONALLY KNOWN

"Yeah, I'm sure. That way I can keep an eye on you and make sure you're safe," he continued.

"Stop the bullshit you two!" Reggie yelled. "I know what's going on. I know y'all fucking. So cut it out."

"What!" I said, trying to act like I was shocked.

"What, nothing. I've noticed how y'all been acting towards each other lately. I can tell how a nigga acts after he gets the pussy."

"Come on now, Reggie, not now," Damian tried to defuse the conversation.

"Whatcha mean, not now?" Reggie turned his attention towards Damian. "Trust me, nigga, I could care less about what y'all are doing. Just don't try to play me like I'm some stupid ass nigga from around the way."

"I wouldn't ever try to play you, dawg. And out of respect for you, I just wanna make sure Naomi is all right. That's all."

Meanwhile, Stone's cell phone rang and after he answered it, his facial expression changed. "All right. We'll handle it on this end," he told the caller and then he hung up the phone. "My guy outside just informed me that about eight FBI agents just hopped out of their cars and they're trying to get into the building right now."

"Oh, shit!" I said. My body was instantly struck with fear. I rushed back to my bedroom, grabbed my duffle bag from the bed and dashed back into the front room.

Reggie had already bolted out of the front door, but Damian stood there and waited for me. He extended his hand. "Come on baby," let's go," he told me.

I took his hand and followed him out the front door. I had no idea where in the hell he planned to take me, so I just followed his lead. "Didn't Stone say they were trying to come through the front door, so where are we going?"

"Reggie said that there was an underground utility basement in the laundry room on the first floor, so we're going down the back staircase to get there."

"What about Stone? What is he going to do?" I continued to question him.

"Don't worry about him. He's going to be fine. He said he'll meet up with us in a few minutes," Damian explained, and then he literally pulled me forcibly down the stairway.

When we reached the bottom floor, Damian heard a loud BOOM. Then the building shook. Debris from the ceiling started falling down around us. Visions of me dying inside of this building engulfed me and my body became numb. But that didn't stop Damian. He dragged me into the laundry room and down the stairs that lead to the basement. The door had already been kicked open by Reggie, so we knew we weren't that far behind him.

The basement was poorly lighted with old light bulbs, but that didn't deter us from finding our way out. The thought of freedom weighed heavily on my heart. I wanted it so badly I could taste it. My mind flashed to prison orange again and I didn't look good in it. I held onto Damian's hand and helped him help me get to freedom.

"Come on, baby, we're almost there," he said. And when I zoomed in ahead of us and noticed that there was indeed light at the end of this tunnel, I began to breathe. The weight of everything around me fell off my shoulders as we approached the half-cracked doorway that lead to the outside. When we finally wiggled our way through it and were able to see that the coast was clear, we fled on foot away from the building and hoped that we'd flag down a cab before the FBI got wind of which direction we ran.

I can't lie, I was dead tired, exhausted to say the least. Reggie was nowhere in sight and that frightened me. But what really frightened me was when I looked back at the building, I noticed that the apartment we had and the entire floor had been blown up and was completely engulfed in flames. My heart sank at the thought that Stone had started an explosion in the apartment and killed himself in the process so that we could escape. This was something you'd see in a fucking movie. There was no way I would've done that for anyone else. Nor did I have the guts to even attempt something of that magnitude. Stone gave new meaning to the word *loyalty*. And he'll be forever in my heart.

We walked five blocks before we caught a cab. Instead of telling the cab driver to take us to the nearest transit station, we told him to take us north towards Connecticut. Thank God he didn't ask us any questions. But he required us to give him cash up front before he moved the car, so we did. And as soon as the cab began to head north, Damian and I were finally able to let out a long sigh.

It had been two weeks since Damian and I left New York. We'd traveled from state to state and stayed out of the public eye. It took about five days before we saw our faces broadcasted on national television, so I panicked the first time I saw it. But Damian reminded me that as long as we had our fake passports and driver's licenses on hand, we were fine.

Periodically, I'd worry about what was going on back in New York. The thought of not being able to speak to my parents bothered me more than not knowing where Reggie was hiding out. I knew he could take care of himself. Since there were no new reports about him being arrested, I knew he was still on the streets. My guess was he was probably sitting on a beach somewhere, sipping on a cold Corona with a slice of lime floating at the top of the bottle. However, when my brand new cell phone rang I got an entirely different story.

Damian was sitting next to me on the hotel bed when the call came through. He and I both looked at each other like we'd just saw a ghost. "Hello," I said, after allowing the phone to ring four times.

"Hey, sis, this is your brother!" Reggie yelled through the phone.

His voice magnified with each word he uttered. He sounded like he was excited about something. But I was even more excited to hear his voice and to know that he was all right. "Oh, my God! I can't believe it's you," I said and then I pressed the speakerphone button so Damian could hear our conversation.

"Yeah, it's me. So, I guess y'all are all right?" he yelled again. There was a lot of loud traffic noise in the background, so I assumed he was either walking or driving with the windows down, which made it very hard for him to hear me.

"Yeah, we're good. And you?"

"Yeah, I'm great. I'm still roaming around the city. I couldn't bring myself to leave after I found out what Stone did for us. Plus, I wasn't going to let Vanessa off the hook after what she did to me. She basically destroyed everything I built."

I placed my hand over my mouth. "Reggie, what did you do?" I forced myself to say.

"Let's just say that she won't be running her fucking mouth anymore. I got that bitch, that nigga Ben and that nigga Dre lit their stinking asses up inside of a house fire."

Shocked by his words, I said, "What!"

Reggie chuckled. "Yeah, I paid that nigga Stone had waiting for us outside to put me up in his crib for a while. Then I got him to help me find out where those motherfuckers were hiding out. And instead of running in the crib and blasting all of them in their fucking heads, me and that cat barricaded all the windows and the front door and set the spot on fire and burned them alive. You should've heard Vanessa screaming when that fire got to her ass. It was like music to my ears."

"Vanessa's dead?"

"Damn right! That bitch and those niggas finally got what they deserved."

"So, what do we do now?" I asked him. Believe it or not, Damian and I needed a plan. I was tired of going from one hotel to the next. And I was sure Damian felt the same way.

"I don't know what to tell you right now. But I do know that coming back to New York isn't the answer, because Marco and Miguel are standing in line behind the Feds. They are looking for us too."

I didn't want to admit it, but I knew there was a chance that Marco would have us on his radar after we lost his shipment to the Feds. So, this was another situation we had to deal with. "What about mom and dad? Have you been able to see or talk to them?" I asked.

"No, I haven't. But I've been able to get money to them though. So don't worry, they're in good hands."

"So, what's next for you?"

"I don't know, baby sis. But I do know that I can't leave New York right now, especially with all the product we have left. I talked to Stone's people and they've agreed to help me get rid of it. And until that mission is completed I'm a sitting duck."

"Don't you think that's a little too risky?"

"Of course it is. But what am I going to do with one and a half million dollars worth of product? Just let it sit in the warehouse and collect dusk? No way. I'm a businessman. And besides that, I got a baby on the way. I couldn't leave Malika either."

"Sounds like you got a lot on your plate," I said.

"Yeah, it looks that way," he chuckled again. "Hey, listen, baby sis, tell Damian I said to take care of you, a'ight?"

"Alright," I managed to say, my voice starting to crack.

"Oh, yeah, and I want you to know that if you ever get word that something happened to me, don't start crying and shit. Just get yourself together and bring your ass back to the city, because I'm gonna have a large amount of cash put away for you and my unborn child. You follow me?"

"Yeah, but how will I know where to find it?"

"Just think back to where we used to play when we were kids. And when you remember the spot, then you'll know where to go from there. Now, I gotta go. I love you."

"I love you too," I assured him.

I sat there on the bed and wondered how my life would play out. I knew I didn't want it to play out in jail and I also knew that I didn't want to end up dead, so I looked at Damian and said, "Do you promise to keep me safe?"

He replied, "What kind of question is that? Of course I will."

INTERNATIONALLY KNOWN: NEW YORK'S FINEST (PART 2)

KIKI SWINSON

I'm My Brother's Keeper

It had been over three months since Damian and I had been on the run and a couple of weeks since we last spoke to Reggie. When we spoke, he acted as if he was a walking time bomb. After we hung up with him I feared that the next call we got from him would be from jail, or even worse, someone else calling to say that he'd been murdered. News like that would definitely take me over the edge for sure.

Reggie and our father, Carter Foxx, were the only two who had our phone number. Damian and I were sharing the same phone. There was no sense in either of us having separate phones. Things had changed momentarily for Damian and I. We were living in Memphis, Tennessee with his half-brother, Champ, while things chilled in New York. Compared to the city, Memphis was slow, but that might have been a good thing. It gave Damian and I time to get to really know each other. He had my back and it made me feel special. I knew I could depend on him through thick and thin. And that was definitely a good thing.

I sat outside on the balcony of a condo apartment Champ owned in downtown Memphis and began to

INTERNATIONALLY KNOWN

daydream. The place overlooked the Mississippi River. It was serene, calming, and very conducive for thinking.

I thought back on the times when life was good. I had just gotten my wings to work with the airlines and soon thereafter my connections to get high potency cocaine were in full effect. Reggie was making tons of cash and I was officially apart of the high mile club. Unfortunately for us, our place at the top of the food chain was short lived. And what was so devastating about the fall from grace was that I had gotten used to the perks that came with the good life. Once you've had a taste of the good life, eating scraps wasn't appetizing at all. So while I stood outside reminiscing on the past events from my life, Damian joined me. He held out our iPhone for me to take it. "Who is it?" I uttered softly.

"It's Foxx," he replied. His tone was different and his facial expression sent me a clear message that something wasn't right. I was somewhat apprehensive about taking the phone from him, but I figured the longer I took to confront the inevitable, the longer it would take to deal with it.

After I hesitated for several seconds, I finally took the phone and said hello. "Chica, I hate to be the one to tell you this, but your brother is missing," my father said.

I wanted to act like I didn't hear him. But there was no denying what he'd just said. Realizing this, my heart sunk and my knees buckled and I was about to fall down to the floor at that moment, but Damian caught me just in time.

"Baby, watch your step," he said as he put a hand on each side of my waist.

I almost dropped the phone but Damian grabbed it before it slipped from my hand and put my father on speakerphone. "Foxx, you there?" Damian asked.

"Yeah, I'm here. Hey, listen, you two, I know this is not the best move but I'm gonna need for you guys to come back East to help me find your brother. And once we get 'em back safely, then we can part ways."

"Do you have any idea where he could be?" Damian pressed the issue.

"One of my sources told me he could be in the hands of Marco and his son, Miguel. But then I heard that Vanessa's people got him because they think he had something to do with her murder."

"Well, don't worry about it Foxx," Damian replied. "We're on our way. And when we make contact, we'll let you know."

After Damian ended the call with my father he looked at me and said, "Let's go. We got to head back to New York."

I looked at Damian with a look of fear. I didn't have a good feeling about this trip and I made him aware of it. "Damian, I'm having a really bad feeling about this," I began to say. "I think we could be walking into a death trap if we go back."

"But what if you're wrong? What if it's not a trap and he really needs us?" Damian tried to reason with me. And as much as I wanted him to be right, my feelings would not change. Reggie was a soldier at heart. He knew the streets like the back of his hands. So I felt if he was really missing, it was his choice. Reggie was the type of man that wouldn't let anyone see him slipping or allow them to get close to him, so I found it very hard to believe that he was in harm's way. Now I may be wrong about all of this, but at that very moment, my heart rode a different wave.

Damian escorted me back into the condo and led me to the bed we shared. I took a seat at the edge of the bed and buried my face in my hand. It didn't take Damian long to lift my head back up. When he looked into my eyes, I was sure they were extremely glassy from the tears that were forming in my eyes. When I blinked, the tears started rolling down my face. Damian stood over me and tried to wipe every tear that fell from my eyes with the back of his hand.

"Stop crying baby, everything is going to be all right," he told me.

"But what if it isn't? What if we go back to New York and something bad happens?" I asked.

"If it does, just let me handle it. I promise I won't let anyone touch one hair on your head," he assured me and then he kissed me in the middle of my forehead.

I sat there and looked at him run his fingers through my hair. A few seconds later, he rubbed my back in a circular motion with the same hand. "I'll die first before I let someone do something to you," he continued as he looked into my eyes.

I remained silent in hopes that everything Damian said would resonate in my heart and my mind. I wished everything would go back the way it was before the Feds came on the scene and wreaked havoc on everything we built. Unfortunately, I was doing a bit of wishful thinking, so I snapped back into reality and decided to let Damian get in the driver's seat. Who knows, maybe he'd be able to do everything he promised? If not, in the end we'll be fucked.

Once I got my emotions back on track I got up from the bed and began to pack a few things into my luggage. I knew Damian wouldn't know how long we'd be in New York, so I took it upon myself to pack one week's worth of clothing just in case our trip was extended. Damian was on the opposite side of the bedroom gathering up his things to pack in his luggage.

"What time are we leaving?" I asked. It was at least eleven hundred miles from Memphis to New York, so I wanted to know what time we were heading out, considering the only option we had to travel was by car. We had bought something less conspicuous, a three-year-old Nissan Maxima. It had some bells and whistles: GPS navigation, CD/DVD player, and a nice sound system. But it wasn't my SUV . . . I really missed driving around the city in my whip.

Damian looked down at his wristwatch. "I wanna get out of here within the next hour," he replied.

It was eleven-thirty in the morning and it was very sunny outside. The temperature had to have been around seventy-five degrees because of the constant breeze I felt when it hit my face. It seemed like the perfect day to travel but when you think about where we had to travel to, the thought alone changed the mood and sent a dark cloud over my head.

"Do you think it would be a good idea for us to drive across country in broad daylight? I mean, we are gonna have to make a couple of stops to get gas and food along the way," I began to explain. Since we had been in Memphis, we had been low-key, chilling out mostly at home. I had cut my hair lower and had been wearing different color wigs. Hell, in Memphis no one paid us any attention besides the occasional old woman or couple telling us how cute we looked as a couple. Plus we had been sporting a lot of sunshades and just that simple accessory alone changed out appearance.

"We own sunshades, right?" he asked.

"Yeah."

"Well, there you go. And besides, no one knows our car and we have new IDs, so we're going to be just fine."

I sighed, "I know I'm being more paranoid than usual. It's just that things have been good since we've been here and I just don't want anything to mess it up." Although Champ was a straight up guy, he knew people with street creds and was able to hook up with a cat who was an underground expert at doing fake IDs. We had passports, new driver's licenses and social security cards.

"It's normal to feel the way you're feeling right now," Damian tried reassuring me. "But at the same time I want you to know that I'm gonna be with you and I will die first before I let something happen to you."

I looked into Damian's eyes and body movements while he poured his heart out to me and he made it perfectly clear about how much he loved me. I needed to hear the sincerity in his voice and he gave it to me. Growing up as a daddy's girl and the baby of the family with Reggie being the oldest, I'd always been sheltered and protected. No one ever had a chance to mess with me as long as my family was around. So, to have Damian around to fill those shoes while my father and Reggie were absent, definitely filled the void.

After Damian and I packed up our things he got on the phone and called his brother, Champ, to let him know of our plans to leave. He didn't go into any details about where we were going, but he did tell him about how long we'd be gone. Immediately after Damian ended their call he grabbed his 9mm Glock from his sock drawer, his sunshades and car keys, and headed to the front door. I followed in his footsteps after I grabbed my handbag and my sunshades.

The moment I stepped foot outside the front door, anxiety hit me squarely in the face. My stomach started rumbling and fear instantly consumed me to the point that I stopped in my tracks. I stood there at the front door like a statue with my handbag across my shoulders and my luggage in one hand.

Damian turned around when he noticed that I wasn't behind him and said, "Babe, what's wrong? Are you okay?"

"I'm scared, Damian," I told him.

Damian put his things in the car and then he walked back to where I was standing. "I told you, I got you, right?"

"Yes," I said, barely audible.

"Well, then, let's go," he said, and then he took my luggage from my hand and grabbed my other hand and escorted me to the car.

New York, here we come . . .

INTERNATIONALLY KNOWN: NEW YORK'S FINEST (PART 2)

KIKI SWINSON

Damian's Point of View

Naomi and I got on the road and headed north. I figured with my driving technique we'd be back in New York in less than sixteen hours. I knew we had to stay under the radar so I kept that in mind while I was behind the steering wheel.

Occasionally, I'd look at Naomi while she stared out of the passenger side window. It was obvious she had a lot on her mind and as much as I wanted to relieve her of all the stress that burdened her, I knew it wouldn't be enough.

Naomi was used to living the life of a single woman, shopping and dating older, Latino mob bosses, and now she's on the run for her life and hiding out from the Feds with me. I've known her for many years and I wanted to be her man for more than half of that time. To have her with me under these circumstances seem somewhat surreal. Okay, granted, I'm a hustler. I've sold drugs damn near all my life, but I also considered myself a good man, and when my heart told me that I was with the right chick, I put plans into action.

When I told Naomi that I'd die for her, I meant that shit. Only real niggas would put their life on the line like that. I learned a long time ago that when you do people right, good shit would come back to you. I just hoped that after she and I found her brother, we could get back out of New York undetected, so we could move forward in our relationship. I'd love to wife her up. But that may be impossible. Thanks to the FBI, our names were circulating through every damn computer database in America. We had what I considered to be damn good IDs with fake names, but if I married Naomi, I wanted it to be using our real names. The names we had called each other since we were young kids.

I thought about leaving the country and getting married on one of those Caribbean islands, but I wasn't sure how Naomi would feel about that. So I stuck that idea on the back burner and figured I bring it up later when the time was right.

Two hours into the drive, Naomi broke her silence and said, "Pull over at this next stop so I can use the bathroom."

When I looked and saw that she wanted me to pull over at a deserted ass service station, I had some reservations. "Can you hold it at least for a couple more miles? That joint looks like some rednecks own it," I commented.

"Well, pull off on the side of the road somewhere, because I've been holding my pee for the last two and a half hours and I'm about to piss on myself."

I hesitated for a moment, debating whether or not I should pull over to this dilapidated gas station. We were still in Tennessee, between Memphis and Nashville, and I was told there were rednecks throughout this area, so I wasn't being paranoid for nothing. "There's a rest stop five miles up the road," I said after I saw the sign.

"Okay, let's get there," she told me.

I pressed down on the accelerator and sped up the road. Through my peripheral vision I saw her tapping her left foot against the floorboard, which was a clear indication that she needed to use the bathroom as soon as possible. Thankfully, it only took me a matter of three minutes to get her to the rest stop. And as soon as I parked the car, Naomi sprang from the car quicker than I could blink my eyes. "Hurry up," I yelled before she closed the car door.

I sat in the car and watched Naomi as she raced towards the women's bathroom. After she disappeared around the corner, I sat there and watched other travelers as they pulled up, got out of their cars and walked around. I couldn't count one black person out of all the people I saw at this rest stop. Naomi and I were definitely in the sticks. White folks ran this area and they seemed proud as they paraded around with confederate flags hanging up in the back window of their trucks.

While I sat in the driver's seat, I saw a redneck state trooper pull up on the left side of me. He drove his patrol car into a parking space two spaces from where I was parked. He got out of his car, grabbed his huge, gray, cop hat from the front seat, placed it on his head and then he closed the car door. He took a couple of steps away from the car and slightly turned around to take inventory of the area around him. Seeing this made me nervous. Not only were Naomi and I on the fucking run from the Feds, I was carrying a loaded 9mm Glock.

I maintained my cool, although a thousand and one thoughts were floating in my head. I wasn't worried about the state trooper asking for ID since we had fake IDs now. But the thought of being recognized was still a possibility. If the trooper did recognize me, I could shoot my way out of here but there were consequences. That being Naomi would get caught up in the crossfire and who knows, she may get hurt if I tried to play Rambo in these backwoods.

After mulling over the idea of possibly playing cops and robbers with that fucking cracker, Naomi walked out of the restroom and began to walk towards the car. I watched her body movement and her reaction when she saw the state trooper standing a few feet away from our car. I also kept watch on the cop from my corner eye. As long as she stayed cool, all would be okay.

The moment she walked by him he opened his mouth and uttered a few words to her. My window was up so I couldn't hear what he was saying. But after I saw Naomi smile and utter a couple of words back to him, I knew their conversation was harmless and let out a sigh of relief. When she got into the car I grilled her immediately. "What did he say to you?"

As long as I've known Naomi, she never wore her seat belt, but she did it today. After she strapped herself in, she sat back in her seat and said, "He just asked me if I was enjoying the weather."

"That's it?"

"Yeah, that was it."

"And what did you say?"

"I told him I hoped it stayed like this," she began to say. Then her tone changed, "Oh shit, he's coming this way," she continued. Her face looked like it was stricken with fear. So my heart started racing at that very moment. I started to turn my attention towards the direction of the state trooper, but Naomi stopped me. "Wait, don't turn around. Just act normal," she instructed me.

I kept my attention on Naomi, and tried to remain calm. "Is he still walking this way?" I asked her.

"Yes, he's coming,"

"Think I should pull off?" I blurted out. I needed to weigh my options and getting bagged up by this cracker wasn't what I had on my agenda.

"No, just sit back in your seat and act like we're having a conversation about where we're gonna eat," she suggested.

But before I could sit back in my seat, the state trooper tapped on the window. I pretended to act shocked that he was there and then I pressed down on the automatic window switch. As the window opened I greeted Him, "Hey sir, how are you doing?"

INTERNATIONALLY KNOWN

"I'm doing great, but you and your missus aren't going to be doing great if y'all continue to ride on that back tire," the state trooper advised me.

As bad as I didn't want to, I drug myself out of the car and took a look at the back tire. And just like he mentioned, the tire was definitely going flat. In fact, I figured if I'd drove another ten miles, I would've ended up driving the car on its rims, fucking up our whip.

"Got a spare in the trunk?" he asked me.

"Yeah, there should be," I replied. I was only about two and a half feet away from him, so my heart was racing. I had my Glock tucked away in the right side of my pants and if I made the wrong move, it would stick out like a sore thumb. Knowing I couldn't bring on that type of heat, I stepped away from the trooper and proceeded to the back of the car. To my surprise the trooper followed me.

"Think you'll need some help?" he asked as he approached me.

I opened the trunk of the car to shield my face. I couldn't afford for him to see my facial expression because I wasn't feeling homeboy. He was getting on my fucking nerves. I mean, when have you ever seen a fucking cop ask a black man if he needs help putting on a spare? Not me. This man was bugging me the fuck out. I wanted to pull out my pistol and tell him to scram. But I knew that wouldn't do me or Naomi any good, so I politely told him no. Unfortunately for me, that didn't do the trick. After I told him I didn't need his help, he stuck around and sparked up a conversation.

"Where are you from son?" he asked. "You don't sound like you're from these parts."

Caught off guard by his question, I froze for a second. Then I came back into the zone when Naomi stepped back out of the car. "Is the tire that bad that we can't drive on it?" she asked immediately after she stepped to the back of the car.

"Yeah, hun, that tire is completely destroyed," the trooper replied. "You guys wouldn't have been able to drive a decent mile before it gave out on you."

I was somewhat happy that Naomi came at the appropriate time to distract the cop, but then I thought about how I would handle the situation if this cracker became suspicious of us and tried to snatch her up. I knew it would be World War III if I had to defend her.

Naomi looked at me, cracked a smile and said, "Do you know what you're doing?"

I forced myself to smile back, hoping he'd put his focus on the joke Naomi cracked on me versus the question about where I was from. "Stand out here long enough and you'll find out," I told her.

The state trooper laughed at how I responded to Naomi. "My wife would've given me the evil eye if I would've talked back to her."

"Trust me, he's sleeping on the sofa tonight," Naomi commented.

I looked at Naomi admiring her way of finding humor in this situation. I knew she hadn't heard when the cop asked me where I was from, but the fact that she came to my aid after she realized the cop wasn't carrying his ass on really said a lot about her. I knew she was one of those chicks who'd stick by her man, but this stunt took her to another level.

It didn't dawn on me immediately but I had to remember that as a flight attendant, Naomi was used to dealing with white folks and other nationalities. She was actually at another level; higher level than Reggie or me. She was the reason we had an international connection when we were the kings of New York.

"Well, I guess I'll leave you love birds alone," the trooper told us.

Seeing this cracker step off and go on about his business almost made me jump for joy. All of the pressure hanging over my head started falling off of me as soon as he stepped away. I looked at Naomi and gave her a quick wink. "You're a lifesaver, baby!" I whispered. "Do you know he asked me where I was from?"

"When did he ask you that?" she whispered back.

"Right before you got out of the car."

"You know what? I sensed that he was saying something out of pocket to you and that's why I got out of the car."

I blew her a kiss. "I owe you for that one, right there."

"You just hurry up and change that fucking tire before he brings his ass back over here," she smiled back at me.

"If you grab the spare from the trunk while I un- screw this jack, we'll be out of here in no time," I continued to speak low. I couldn't let that man hear our conversation for nothing in the world. He'd already asked me where I was from. But luckily for me, Naomi intercepted his mission and diverted his attention away from me. She scored major points for that shit. And she would be rewarded in due time.

After I changed the tire, Naomi and I got back into the car and left the rest stop before that cop realized who we were. Before we jetted on his ass, we saw him harassing other people who were parked near his patrol car.

INTERNATIONALLY KNOWN:
NEW YORK'S FINEST (PART 2)

KIKI SWINSON

Naomi's Role In This Shit

Damian and I got back on the road and continued to head northeast, towards our destination. After that scare at the rest area, I really didn't want to stop anywhere else. That close encounter we had with that state trooper was a once in a lifetime thing. The next time we run into a cop, it would be our luck that the motherfucker would know who we were and we couldn't chance that.

I was still paranoid and I was sure Damian was too. We had new IDs and new names, and the best thing we could do was keep our cool. That was easy for me to think, but hard to control. But I kept my cool and that was a good thing. If we had to encounter cops on our trip, I hope we both maintained our control and cool, and trust that our fake IDs were good enough.

I was pissed I didn't put on one of my wigs before leaving Memphis. Damian was bald now. A look I had to get used to when he first shaved his head. Additionally, where he used to have just a mustache, he now had long sideburns that connected to a well-groomed beard. He already had my heart for being my black knight in shining armor, but damn, I never knew the man would look as fine as he did after he shaved his head. Hell, I didn't even know I was attracted to baldheaded men.

He struck up a conversation and told me he had forgotten for a quick minute how I was used to being around people of all races and walks of life, and he liked how I handled the white state trooper. He talked about how Reggie had told him a long time ago that he needed me in the business because I could make the connections with other races of people that he and Damian couldn't.

The more I listened to Damian, the more I realized that I did make a difference in this crazy ass game we played. I was the power broker for those at the airport who worked for us as well as I was the one who brought Marco in.

I dozed off after the stop at the rest area and my mind drifted to when Reggie and I were small kids. Even then we were close. I grew up idolizing my big brother. He grew up watching over and protecting me. Although I would go to City College at the insistence of my dad, it didn't change our relationship. Reggie was the one who encouraged me to make connections with people of all nationalities and taught me to use those connections. Internally, I smiled because my big brother had groomed me to be the person I was today. I loved my parents immensely, but I realized my brother was responsible for making me a queen.

Now it was time for me to pay him back. *To be my brother's keeper.* I took that shit seriously. Regardless of the circumstances, I had his back . . . and I was determined to bring him home alive.

INTERNATIONALLY KNOWN

Our phone ringing brought me out of my stupor. Force of habit made me look at the caller ID, but it could only be one of several people: Foxx, Reggie or Damian's half-brother, Champ. Secretly, I was hoping it was Reggie. No such luck, it was Foxx.

"Hello," I said.

"Hey, Chica, you guys on the road yet?" my dad asked.

"Yeah, dad, we left a little while ago," I was tentative telling Foxx what time we left, because I was still disoriented from waking up. I looked at Damian and he gave me a quick glance but his focus was on the road. I don't know how long I had fallen asleep, but it was one of those sleeps that had you more tired than you were before you fell asleep.

"What time do you think you guys will make it here?" Foxx continued his questioning.

"Hold on, daddy, let me ask Damian," I responded. Before I could ask the question, Damian was already lip-syncing me an answer. "About eight hours. We had a minor setback. One of the back tires was low on air and Damian replaced it at a rest area in Tennessee. But we are making good time now." I felt myself coming around. I looked at the clock on the dashboard and it read seven forty-seven. I kind of laughed to myself, thinking about the number 747 aircraft I had flown on when I was a flight attendant. For the first time I realized how much I missed that life. And all the time I thought I wanted out of the flight attendant business, now I wanted back in. This shit is crazy.

I was now in listening mode as my dad told me what was up with Reggie's situation. He said he's tried to call Reggie's phone over two dozen times with no success. Apparently, he wasn't sure who had Reggie. Word on the street wasn't one version but several different versions of who snatched up my brother. The logical choice was Marco and his son, Miguel. The other version was Vanessa's family members, and lastly, the one word was Dre's crazy ass cousins from South Carolina. My first thought was anyone else except Dre's psycho two cousins. Reggie had hired them on several occasions to handle some wet work duty for him, and these psychos were happy to kill for money. Those grizzly motherfuckers loved killing for free, so money was an added incentive.

My father went on to tell me he wanted us to go to an address in New Jersey. I had the phone on speaker, so I put the address in the GPS navigation system. Damian wanted to know who lived there and my dad informed us it was one of Stone's hideaways. The phone got quiet for several seconds and I knew what it was about. My father missed his best friend, Big Joey Stone. The man had given his life for his best friend's kids and although my dad had brothers and sisters, Stone was the one who was the closest to him in the world, besides our mom.

"You guys will be safe there," my dad continued. "We have to play this carefully and safely. I don't want anything happening to you guys. Plus, I'm working on something else that I will tell you guys about when y'all get here."

"How is mom?" I asked. Once again the phone got quiet. "Dad . . ." I raised up in the seat. I felt a frog in my throat. Something wasn't right. Being the baby of the family, my dad and Reggie tried to shelter me from the realities of life. They figured I couldn't handle the streets like they did, so I had to prove myself through the years. My dad used to be in the streets hard. And when he decided to retire he took Reggie under his wings and groomed him to take over. I was fascinated by their lifestyle and wanted to be apart of it. And in order to be down I had to prove myself. So, I proposed the opportunity for them to get major weight through men I met during my flights with the airlines. In the beginning, they thought that I was in over my head. But after they saw how solid my connections were, I became apart of their operation.

"Well . . . well, she found out about Reggie," he finally said. I was even more worried now. My mom didn't get involved in our craziness. Since all of this madness had transpired, she had put her trust in my father that everything was good.

"Reggie had been sending us packages every week on a Saturday," he continued. "Mostly money and a gift and letter for your mother. Well, we didn't get a package this past weekend. And today is Monday and there's still no money, gift or a letter for your mother. So to make sure everything was all right, I got on the phone to reach out to him and his phone went straight to voicemail. I called him so many times I lost track. I even texted him and I still got no reply. And you know your mother. She can sense when something is wrong. And as I told you before, the FBI came around several times in the first month after you guys left. And every time they stopped by she would go into another part of the house and leave me alone to speak with them. And after they left, she never once questioned me. But now the game has changed. She wants this situation handled and handled quickly."

"Damn, dad, what the fuck? How come you didn't write mom a letter and give her a gift . . . pretend you were Reggie?"

"Dammit, Naomi, I didn't know the protocol," he answered.

"What do you mean you didn't know the protocol?"

"I didn't know how Reggie was sending us the package. Your mother was the one receiving the package. Reggie was sending it directly to her. Apparently, Reggie was giving the packages to our mailman, who he knows personally, and in turn the mailman would give the package to your mother."

"Shit," was the only thing I could say.

"You guys get here safely and go directly to that address, and I will see you guys soon," my dad said.

"Foxx, what's the other thing about?" Damian asked.

"No, we will talk about that when you guys get here. Be safe, love you guys."

"Love you too daddy," I said weakly.

I was officially worried now.

My dad was concerned.

INTERNATIONALLY KNOWN:
NEW YORK'S FINEST (PART 2)

KIKI SWINSON

Damian's Turn to Talk

The second after Naomi and I got off the phone with her father, she turned her head to stare out of the passenger window once again. I touched her on her shoulders and got her attention. "What's on your mind?" I asked her. In one respect, I was asking her a stupid ass question. But with women, you could never tell what was on their mind.

She turned towards me. "I'm just worried about my mother." she told me.

"Look at it this way, when we find your brother and bring him home, she'll get back to her normal self."

Naomi sighed. "It's all my fault."

"No it's not. Don't ever say that again."

"I've got to. Let's keep it real, Damian," she began to say. "If I wouldn't have introduced Reggie to all my connects, none of this shit would've happened. He was fine being a low level supplier. But no, I had to prove myself to him and my father by showing them they could take their operation global. And because of it, you and I are on the run for our freedom and for our lives, and my parents are worried too death, Vanessa is dead and my brother is now missing. Now tell me what else can go wrong?"

"Baby, don't do this to yourself. None of this is your fault."

"Then who's fault is it Damian?"

"Naomi, shit happens. So, don't beat yourself up about it."

Instead of commenting she tried to place her face in the palm of her hands. I saw the pain in her expression so I grabbed the bottom of her chin, lifted her face back up and turned it around so she could face me. "Your brother and your father would be really upset with you right now if they knew you blamed yourself for everything that's going on. We live in a world where niggas have no loyalty at all. They are sheisty, they're cowards, they don't have respect for themselves and they'll kill their own family. So, why even blame yourself when none of this shit is your fault?"

"You just don't understand."

"You're right, I don't. The shit that happened to your brother could've happened to anyone. And besides, we don't even know who has him. It could be anybody."

"But what if we find out he's dead? What if his body is floating in the Hudson River?"

"That's not going to happen?"

"What if it does?" she pressed the issue. It was obvious how she was conditioning her mind for the worse case scenario. And as much as she could've been right, it was my duty to make light of the situation. I couldn't let her fall apart. I had to keep her

level headed until I got her back to New York. I knew
that's what her father would want. And that's exactly
what I intended to do.

"Will you stop talking like this?" I begged her.

"I'm just trying to figure out who has my brother. And I won't be able to rest my mind until I get a
clear answer."

"Well, you aren't gonna get it here."

She ignored my comment and said, "I will go
fucking crazy if I found out Vanessa's people got him.
I mean, the only people he had beef with was
Vanessa's people and Miguel. And if anyone had a
motive to kidnap him, it would be them. Everybody
else in the hood wouldn't dare fuck with him."

"Why don't you calm down and take this time to
get yourself some sleep. And when we get back to the
east coast, we'll find the answers to all of your questions." I instructed her and then I tapped her on her left
thigh.

I knew Naomi was afraid to go back to New
York. She was even more afraid to find out that Reggie could possibly be dead. I understood where she
was coming from. I lost my cousin Justin to the streets
six years ago. He was delivering some product to one
of the spots we had and before he could get in the
building, four niggas robbed him for everything he had
and then they shot him eight times. I thought I'd never
get over that night, but I did. And if by chance, Reggie ran into that same fate, I promised I'd be there to
help Naomi get through it.

After I convinced Naomi to get some rest, she rested her head against the headrest. She turned her head to face the scenery outside and then she tuned everything around her out and closed her eyes.

INTERNATIONALLY KNOWN

INTERNATIONALLY KNOWN:
NEW YORK'S FINEST (PART 2)

KIKI SWINSON

Naomi's Trip to New Jersey

In my dream I was a commando, dressed in military camouflage clothing as if I was some warrior bitch in an overhype movie. I was walking out of the Atlantic Ocean strapped with guns and grenades all over my body, and in my hands I was carrying a military-issued M-4 rifle. I had grown up shooting different guns. My Uncle Stone taught me and Reggie what we needed to know about shooting. My father wasn't a gunman. But Stone told us my father was probably a better shooter than him.

But I didn't like guns. It didn't stop me from knowing how to use multiple weapons . . . it just wasn't my cup of tea. Hence, that's why I didn't understand the dream. But there I was dripping wet with water walking towards a big ass warehouse that I was sure housed my brother. Like I said, some warrior bitch shit out of a fucking movie.

The door of the warehouse flew open and it looked like a hundred or more guerrillas, also dressed in military garb, came running out with rifles of their own shooting at me. I continued walking but now I was returning fire and I could see my enemies falling one by one. I continued my pace. For everyone I shot, it seemed like two or three more guerrillas took the fallen enemy's place. I dropped my clip and reloaded and when I did that I heard gunfire on each side of me. When I looked over it was Stone and Damian dressed like me returning fire. The closer we got to the guerrillas, the more they fell.

After killing what seemed like hundreds of guerrillas and walking over their bodies to get to the door of the warehouse, I saw them, Marco and Miguel. Sitting in a chair, tied up was Reggie. He had duct tape over his mouth, his hands were behind his back, his ankles were tied with rope and rope was around his torso. He looked like he was tied pretty firmly to the chair. Marco had a gun to his head, standing on Reggie's right side. Miguel was standing on his left side with an assault rifle pointed at me. Flanked by both men were other guerrillas with assault rifles also pointed at us.

Marco smiled. That shit eating smile I despised. No words were spoken. I looked at Reggie again and I could see he was beaten pretty damn good. I could feel my adrenaline increasing. I wasn't upset. I was mad. Rage flowed through my veins. I wanted blood. More blood than we had already spilled.

Then it happened. The surprise. From behind us, the guerrillas we had already killed were standing behind us. Bloody, their bodies rippled with holes. When I turned back around, Miguel was two feet away from me, with his gun pointed at my head. When he pulled the trigger, I woke up from my nightmare.

Waking up from my nightmare was perfect timing as Damian was pulling up in the driveway of this

nice, two-story house. It was a subdivision in
Teaneck, New Jersey, probably a good hour from our
old stomping grounds in New York, depending on the
traffic. The yard was big, with beautiful dark green
grass. On the curve sat a vintage 1980 Oldsmobile
Ninety-Eight, white with a burgundy vinyl top.

I knew the owner of such a car. It used to belong
to Big Joey Stone. I had never been to the resident,
but rumor had it that Stone owed about five houses in
the New York – New Jersey areas. To my understand-
ing, they were all nice. He rarely drove the Oldsmobile, but when he did, it turned heads. I figured maybe
because it was in tiptop shape. The car still looked as
if he had just drove it off the dealer's lot.

I looked at the clock on the dashboard and it read
six o'clock. I wasn't sure if that was Eastern or Central
time. I didn't know if Damian had changed the time or
not. When I looked at the cell phone, it read the same
thing, which meant it was Eastern time.

The front door of the house was open and I could
smell bacon, eggs and toast. Before we could ring the
doorbell, my dad opened the screen door and I was
greeted with a big hug. It was a long hug . . . neither
one of us wanted to let go. When we finally pulled
away, he held me at arm's length and just looked at
me.

"You lost some weigh, young lady," he said.

I smiled. "Yes, daddy, I did. I don't know how
eating all of that barbeque and good ass Southern
cooking, but I did manage to lose a couple of pounds
here and there."

"Probably from stressing," Damian added. The two men gave each other some dap and embraced in a man's hug. It was quick and dirty. Although it didn't seem like anything special, it meant a lot to both men.

"Come on, I just finished cooking," my dad stated. "Let's go break bread."

Entering the house, I was amazed. The front door opened into the living room. After descending three stairs, the sunken living room was huge. The nice beige sectional sat in front of a huge entertainment center. In most houses, the entertainment center would be a wall-to-wall unit. In Stone's house, it took up the living room. Adjoined to the living room was the dining room, which included an eight-seat dining room table. It had to be the nicest table I had ever laid eyes on.

After washing our hands in the kitchen sink, which I also fell in love with the kitchen, the three of us sat at the table and ate without talking. The way we were devouring food, Damian and I were hungry. Like my mom, my father could cook his but off in the kitchen. We both had turkey bacon and sausage, the eggs had cheese in them, he had thrown in grits with cheese and white butter, plus regular toast and cinnamon toast. And the three of us devoured every damn morsel of food on that table.

After we ate and put the dishes in the kitchen, my dad showed us the whole house. I was really impressed with not only the house but the collection of furniture and paintings and other trinkets throughout the house. He told us that Stone had put this together all by himself. From scoping out the house, you would have thought it was a woman who had hooked up the furniture, curtains and everything else.

Damian and I were situated in a spare bedroom, which could have easily passed for the master bedroom in most homes in America. We had our own bathroom and I couldn't wait to jump in the shower and get some sleep, even though I had slept most of the way on the long car trip. But I was sure Damian was tired and needed some sleep.

My father told us to get prepared and meet him downstairs before we went to sleep. I didn't like the sound of it, but business was business. And the business at hand was finding Reggie.

When we reached downstairs, my father was settled on the sectional watching the news. That was one of his past times, watching national and local news. He was down with the politics and the local scene in both New York and New Jersey. What he didn't get from the news, he got from the streets. The man loved the streets and the streets loved him.

The sectional was big. Damian and I sat on one side of the sectional while he sat more to the middle. He turned off the TV and just looked at us for a minute or two. No words were spoken. I couldn't read his eyes either. I didn't have a clue what was on my father's mind.

"Naomi, you are my daughter and I love you," he began. I didn't like the tone in his voice but I didn't say anything. He sounded as if he was about to chastise me and I had already told Damian that whatever he had to say, I would listen to it.

"I initially told Reggie I didn't want you involved in his shit. I didn't mind him getting into the drug business, and as a father, that was probably one of my biggest mistakes, not talking my son out of doing something stupid. Doing something lethal." My father paused and I could feel his pain, his hurt. He loved us and the last thing he wanted to do was bury one of his own. He had told us that on many occasions . . . and we had lied that he never would. Hopefully, it wasn't a lie.

"But when you got in, it became a thing of you learning and keeping that attitude in check. I have told you Naomi on many occasions to think before you do or say something stupid or idiotic. That's a sign of being a great leader. You have to be courageous. The business you, Reggie and Damian chose is a dangerous game. . . I always told you guys that. Now you see that when you're not careful, you could lose your arms, your legs or even your life."

He stopped again and I looked at my father hard. I wanted to know what was going on. I didn't mind him chastising me but something was up, I could feel it. Before I could ask him what it was, he continued on with his oration.

"The Feds have been trying to weigh me down to give them the goods about where y'all ran off to. They even threatened to lock me and your mother up if they found out we were funding you guys to stay off the radar. I found out they have all of our phones tapped, which is why I used those throwaway phones to contact you with."

"I hate the fucking Feds! They make my skin crawl! How dare they threaten you and mom like that? That's not constitutional is it?" I spat. I instantly became livid after my father told me how badly the Feds had been harassing them. They hadn't done anything wrong. My father turned the operation over to Reggie and I years ago. Fucking pigs!

"Listen baby girl, let me handle them. I want you and Damian to focus on finding out who has your brother. Time is of the essence right now so that should be your only mission."

"Where do you think we should start?" I questioned my father.

Damian answered for him. "I have a couple of contacts I can reach out to. Maybe we can start there."

"No, that can be risky," my father injected. "You've got to be selective about who you talk to. Remember the Feds are on high alert and my bet is that they've reached out to everyone you know. And if you screw around and contact one of them, there's a huge chance that their phones maybe tapped. Or even worse, they could turn you in for the reward money that's been put out there. After you guys left Reggie went underground so he could stay under the radar and because of that he lost all of his spots. There's a gang of niggas out there and they took over. Every building you guys had locked down are now ran by those cats. So, if you decide to go out there be on the lookout. I heard they're loose cannons and they'll kill you on the spot."

Listening to my father warn us about those niggas carried me back to my nightmare. I was a fucking warrior bitch girl trying to get my brother back and I had Damian and my uncle, Big Joey Stone by my side.

The only problem with that dream.....Stone was dead and gone.

"Dad, we weren't planning to go back to Harlem."

"Foxx you know I'm not new to this. Going back to Harlem wasn't an option. I would be a complete idiot to show my face around there. I know there's niggas in the city who would love to rat me out to the Feds, but I wouldn't give them that opportunity. I have a person who owes me a huge favor and I will bet my life that he hasn't spoken to the Feds. And he's going to be able to help me get around the streets undetected."

"Well, all I can say about it is, you be careful."

"I've got everything under control Foxx."

"What am I going to do in the meantime?" I asked. It seemed like everybody had a plan of their own, but me.

"You're gonna be with me." Damian spoke up.

"Yes Chica, you've got to stick with Damian. The Feds are all over me and if they get the slightest hint that you maybe somewhere near, then everything we've worked for will crash and burn."

Before I could comment, my father's cell phone rang. Damian and I looked at him and froze. We already knew we had to be silent while my father spoke to the other caller, so as soon as he answered it we sat back on the couch like church mice.

My father's call didn't last very long. He uttered a couple of incomplete sentences like, "Are you sure? When did he say that? Well, if you hear anything different, call me at once." And immediately after he ended the call Damian and I sat back up and gave him our undivided attention. "Well, I guess we can cross Vanessa's people off the list." My father announced.

"Why do you say that? Who was that? And what did they say?" I wanted to know.

"Yeah, who was that?" Damian chimed in.

"One of my sources. He just found out that Vanessa's people doesn't have Reggie. In fact, the day before Reggie was taken, the Narcs raided Vanessa's brother's marijuana spot and arrested everyone who was there. And now knowing this, it would be impossible for them to have him."

"How reliable is your source?" Damian asked my father.

"Oh son, he's very reliable," my father assured him.

"Have you spoken with Malika?" I asked. "I mean, she is pregnant with his baby. So, she must know something."

"Your mother has spoken with her and I'm told that she's worried too. You know she can have that baby any day now."

"Damn, I wish I could talk to her. I know she's gotta know something."

"No, she doesn't know anything. The last time she said she spoke to Reggie was a couple of hours before he disappeared. She said, he called her on a secured line and told her that he had to meet someone and when he was done, he would call her back. But it never happened."

"Has the Feds contacted her?" I wondered aloud.

"Yes as a matter of fact they have. But as of lately she hasn't told them anything."

"Daddy, how can you be so sure?" my questions continued.

"I'm not sure. But I figured if they had, they wouldn't keep harassing me."

"Does she know about Vanessa's murder?"

"Yes, she mentioned it once. But I cut her off."

"What did she say?" I probed him.

"She didn't say much. She did mention that she heard about the fire and that it was tragic how Vanessa burned too death in the house fire. And I simply agreed with her and ended the conversation by saying that I heard her death was contributed by some young guys playing a prank."

"Do you think she believed you?" I asked.

"It didn't matter if she believe me or not. I knew my phone was bugged so I said the first thing that came to mind in an effort to throw the Feds off track. It was important for me to play the dumb role and that's what I did."

"I know I shouldn't be saying this, but that bitch got what she deserved. My brother was good to her.

And no matter how much he gave her, she wanted more."

"Look, sweetheart, I know you're upset. But—"

"But nothing daddy! Vanessa destroyed our family. She started this whole fucking investigation. She snitched us all out. She told the Feds about every kilo of cocaine and heroin we brought in from South America and across the Mexico – America border, and the death of the airport worker, Evan Molinas, didn't help. She literally sold us out because she found out that Reggie was having an affair with Malika and that they were about to have a baby. She caused all this turmoil we're going through. So, she deserved to burn in that fire."

"Calm down baby," Damian said as he placed his arm around my shoulder. He saw how upset I was becoming and he knew I could blow a fuse in any minute.

"I'm sorry Damian, but I can't calm down. My brother could be out there somewhere in a warehouse begging for his life while we're here talking about the ungrateful bitch that caused all of this mess in the first place. I'm so mad right now, I could scream. I mean all I want is for this to be over with so we can go back to living life like everyone else. I'm sick and tired of being on the run. Do you know that I wake up every freaking morning, wondering will this be my last day of freedom? Who wants to walk around with that much pressure on their shoulders every waking moment of their life? I'm about to have a nervous breakdown if something doesn't change."

"Naomi," Foxx said my name and just looked at me. He looked angry and he gave off this vibe that I had rubbed him the wrong way. I sat there quietly and waited for him to release his wrath on me. "I understand you're hurt but you need to get that fucking attitude in check. You, my dear, was the one who ignited the whole Reggie and the baby situation when you opened up your mouth and told Vanessa that Malika was pregnant. You threw the gas on the fire and now here we are trying to pick up the pieces so we can fix this shit!"

Wow I was taken aback at how my father ripped me a new asshole. I felt like shit. I was daddy's little angel and he never talked to me like that. And sadly, it was all so matter-of-factly for him. In my selfishness, I had forgotten about that time when Reggie was in the hospital for his gun shot wounds and Vanessa had gotten underneath my skin and in retaliation I let the cat out the bag about my brother's mistress' pregnancy. Vanessa already had a long track record of being messy so while I thought I'd only hurt her, I fucked around and gave that bitch ammunition to destroy my family. Me and my big mouth.

"Well, we're not gonna make anything change sitting here," Damian blurted out.

"Hey, you're right. So, I'm gonna get out of here and let you two do what you do." My father said and stood to his feet. "Oh before I go, I forgot to mention that I have a guy who'll be able to arrange for you two to get new IDs and passports if necessary."

INTERNATIONALLY KNOWN

"We already came equipped. My half-brother took care of us back in Memphis." Damian said.

"Well, you know you can never have too many." My father told him.

"I'll keep that in mine." Damian assured him.

My father didn't hug or kiss me on the cheek before he left. That was not a good sign.

That was not a good feeling.

INTERNATIONALLY KNOWN: NEW YORK'S FINEST (PART 2)

KIKI SWINSON

Damian Calls in a Favor

Naomi and I watched Foxx as he made his exit from the house. And after the front door closed, I called my connect. Naomi stood by as I called in my favor. "Hey Jimmy, I need to see you brother." I said.

"Don't think that'll be a good idea with all the heat on you." Jimmy replied.

"Believe me, I understand where you're going with this but I wouldn't have called you if I thought I'd be drawing heat to you." I began to explain.

I thought Jimmy would've commented by now, but I got complete silence on the other end. "Hey listen Jim, you have a right to be skeptical but I need you to know that I would never put you in a position that would cause you any grief."

"Are you close by?" he finally said.

"I can be," I assured him.

"Well, meet me at my usual spot in thirty minutes."

"I just drove a long ways to get here so if you'll give me an hour to get myself to together, I can come right after that."

"Handle your business and call me in the morning."

INTERNATIONALLY KNOWN

"A'ight, but can you check on something for me?"

"What is it?"

"I'm looking for my brother-in-law." I said and looked at Naomi's face to see her expression. I wanted her to know that I looked at her and her family as my family now. "His name is Reggie Foxx. I just got word that he's been missing for a few days so I need to know if anybody on the streets know of his whereabouts."

"Come see me tomorrow and I might have something for you," Jimmy said.

"Okay, I'll call you in the morning and then we can go from there." I told him.

Immediately after I hung up with Jimmy, Naomi realized that I was in for the night and told me she was going to take a shower and get ready for bed. I told her I'd see her when she was done showering.

While Naomi was in the bathroom I thought back to the first time I got me some pussy. My first sexual encounter was at age sixteen. The girl in my life was actually a woman . . . the best friend of my mom. Her name was Lydia and she looked like a Lydia—plain, average looking and unpretentious. But what Lydia lacked in looks, she made up for in emotional display when it came to me.

Lydia and my mom, Peggy, had been friends since they were kids. My mom was the wild one, while Lydia was grounded, serious and about business. When my mom became pregnant with me at age sixteen, it was her best friend, Lydia, who came to her rescue and helped Peggy out . . . which included babysitting and raising me, while Peggy maintained her wild ways.

Although I looked at Lydia as an aunt, on my sweet sixteenth birthday, she had a different kind of gift for me. When I came home from school, she came in my bedroom and told me she knew I had a crush on the Latina girl, Naomi, and she was going to teach me how to get her. She unzipped my pants and gave me the best present a boy ever had. Then she demanded me to get on my knees so she could teach me what would be my greatest gift to women.

Of course, I was hesitant. But I trusted Lydia so when she put my face between her legs and told me everything to do with my mouth and tongue, I realized something—Lydia was right. That day changed my life when it came to pleasing women. I fucked the shit out of Lydia that day, but it was the things she taught me to do with my tongue that set the stage for me to be the great lover I became.

Naomi had just gotten out of the shower and was just staring at the huge mirror. I could feel her stress and I felt bad for her. Hell, I felt bad for both of us. But this was about her. And I knew what she needed at that moment.

She needed me, and my gift of love. From the time I knew what sex was all about, just being around the woman made my dick hard. All of those years of not being with her had made these past several months terrific. My greatest desire was to please her. And seeing her butt ass naked staring in the mirror, feeling down on her luck, I knew what I had to do.

Naomi was so deep in thought she really didn't pay any attention to me coming into the bathroom. I got on my knees behind her and slid my hands over her nice, smooth perfect ass. I kept that up as I kissed the inside of her thighs. She didn't moan but I could feel her body relax and I knew she was getting into it.

I lived for this moment.

I don't know how long I did this but it seemed to do the trick. Naomi arched her back and pushed her ass out. I flicked my tongue on her clit and started doing my thing. I licked and lightly bit her clit, and occasionally fucked her pussy with my tongue. Naomi was going crazy as I speeded up my pace and then slowed down my rhythm. I kept this technique going for a good fifteen or twenty minutes.

I noticed she couldn't figure out what to do with her hands. At times she would put one hand on the back of my head and made sure my head stayed in that position. Others times she would put both hands on the basin counter as if she was holding on for dear life.

The first time she came she pushed her ass back hard into my face and put her hand on the back of my head. I was wearing that pussy out with my tongue and mouth. Plus, what added to the stimulation was my nose pushing against her asshole.

Sometimes I would re-position my head with my face facing up and chewing on her thick pussy lips, while putting my thick index finger in her asshole. This was one of many positions that drove her crazy.

When she started bucking and fucking my face and putting both hands on the back of my head, I knew she was coming again. Then time harder and stronger.

After she came, she was spent but she knew what time it was. She pushed me down on the rug in front of the basin and she wanted to give me head but this was all about her. I pulled her on top of me and she bucked wild. She was on a mission now and that was to make me come. My dick was super hard—all bone. And that's what I done to my true love—boned the shit out of her.

We were in a smooth and nice rhythm. I loved this position, being on the bottom and pumping my ass off, while Naomi was matching my rhythm with her rhythmic movements. We were going at it like raging animals. I could feel my dick growing inside of her. Occasionally, Naomi would lean down and kiss me. Other times I would bring those nice, firm breasts to my mouth and suck on her pert nipples.

This was my pussy and since the days of slavery, black men have fucked the shit out of their women. Our way of saying, "baby, everything is okay."

I'm a man of many positions. Tonight, this was about pleasing Naomi and releasing her stress. I was doing my thing and I saw the ecstasy on Naomi's face. This was what the doctor order and I was the *remedy*. When she came again, I grunted ecstasy as well.

We stayed on the floor of the bathroom for at least thirty minutes. Naomi lying on top of me was a position we were used to. Me consoling Naomi was a way of life for us now. Ever since we had ran from

New York, we had become closer, and being there for each other was our thing now.

We had to depend on each other, now more than ever. We had to have each other's back.

After we made love, we went to bed. Sex really was the remedy because both of us slept sound, like a sleep depraved couple on the run, which we officially were. I woke the next morning with one thing in mind, getting Jimmy back on the phone.

"Are you up?" I asked him.

"Of course I am."

"Is this a good time for you?"

"It couldn't get any better."

"Can I bring someone?"

"No, you know I don't roll like that. I'm already taking a chance with you."

"Understood. I'll see you in forty-five." I replied and then I disconnected the call. After I shoved my phone back into my pocket, I looked at Naomi and said, "How do you feel staying here until I come back?"

"Do I have a choice?" she replied sarcastically.

"You know I would've taken you if I could. But you know how it is when niggas think everybody is the police."

"Listen, you don't have to go into all of that. I completely understand. Remember I'm not a stranger to all of this either. And at this point I'm down for whatever, especially if it means that it could get us the answers we need concerning Reggie. But all I ask is that you be extra careful and not to take a long time to come back."

"I won't baby. I promise." I told her. And then I handed her the cell phone she and I shared. I figured it would be better if she had it. I could call her from anywhere since I was going to be mobile.

"No, you take it. What am I going to do with it? I mean it's not like I'm going to be able to call you." She reasoned.

"I know, but if I took it I wouldn't be able to call you." I began to explain to her. "I'm gonna be out and about, so I can stop at any of the corner shops and pick up a throwaway phone."

"All right, but when you do it, call me so I can have the number."

"Sure thing," I said. I kissed her on the lips and left.

It felt kind of weird to leave Naomi behind. Since this whole operation blew up in our faces, she and I had been together. There was no separating us. And now that I'm back on the east coast things seemed different. I'm more on the edge and I see that I'm going to have to look over my back a little more than I did when I was in Memphis. I just hoped that this ride I was about to take yielded some information and got us closer to getting Reggie back.

I would never say anything to Naomi, but Reggie should have his ass kicked and kicked good for keeping his ass in New York. It was stupid of him to put himself in that position as well as putting us in that position.

INTERNATIONALLY KNOWN

Naomi wanted normalcy but it was hard to tell her that our lives would never be normal again. I knew there was chance we could beat the drug charge considering Vanessa was the Feds main witness and now she can't talk because she's out of the picture indefinitely. The only thing that loomed over our head was the death of the airport worker. But then I figured that if we hired the right attorney the murder indictment would be thrown out as well. Who knows, maybe the attorney could also pen the body in Reggie's apartment on Stone since he was no longer in the picture. I was all about maximizing every possibility. And if it meant shifting the weight to the grave, then so be it.

Getting the chance to ride around New Jersey again was somewhat surreal. Although it was daylight out, I didn't have to worry much about the cops spotting me. The cops in Teaneck and Hackensack weren't as plentiful as those in any borough of New York. Plus, my baldhead actually changed my look. Even if a cop had a picture of me in his squad car, it wouldn't match my new look. And the sunshades made a difference.

I only had to drive a couple blocks from the house Foxx had set us up in to find a corner store that carried the throwaway phones. I parked my car in an alley and ran into the store. I didn't want to double park and have some car trip with my out-of-state plates. It took no time at all to get the phone and the phone card that came with it. And before I knew it, I was in and out of the store in less than two minutes. On my way out of the store, this Puerto Rican chick approached me. She was phat ass hell. She looked like Rosie Perez in her former days. She had ass like her too. And the tight ass jeans she wore made her more pleasing to the eye. My dick was getting aroused by the second.

She smiled at me and said, "Somebody told me you were looking for me."

I smiled back at her. "Nah baby, you got me mixed up with someone else." I told her.

"What a shame. Because you and I could've had a good time." she replied.

"I'm sure we could've." I commented and then I got back into my car. I looked back at her as I drove away from the corner and thought about how many niggas she told that same line to. She was definitely a knockout. But I knew she had a lot of miles on her pussy. And a nigga like me ain't down with that type of party. So, she can keep it moving.

I had to meet Jimmy at his usual spot in Hoboken. Jimmy was an old head with plenty of money. Some say he's a multi-millionaire. He used to be in the streets but he retired after he lost his wife.

It was then when I met Jimmy. During his grief, he was at a local liquor store in Harlem getting something to drink. His mind was elsewhere and two cats tried to rob him off. I don't know why I stopped the two, but Jimmy felt indebted to me ever since.

"What's up, big Jim," I said to Jimmy as he sat behind his desk playing solitaire on his computer. His spot in Hoboken was an old garage that fixed all types of vehicles. From the outside the place looked like an old rundown chop shop. But inside the place had the most up-to-date equipment. Jimmy's office was upstairs, on the second floor of the garage. From his office he could look down and see everything.

"I hope you didn't bring any heat with you," Jimmy commented. He was serious. Jimmy didn't play any games. And he kept his circle tight. He went through a good year and a half of grieving after his wife died, but then went back to his old self. I didn't know him before his wife died. But those who knew Jimmy used to have mad stories about the crazy shit Jimmy used to get into. He was one of the original gangsters back in his time. He had a slew of hos and he sold mad dope. From what I heard, his operation was so tight, he managed to elude every government agency that tried to take him down. So I couldn't blame him for being skeptical to see me, especially since he had a lot to lose.

"Don't worry, I'm clean. The Feds don't even know that I'm town." I assured him.

"Don't be so sure." Jimmy replied sarcastically.

"Oh, I'm sure." I shot back. I had to make Jimmy believe that I was clean and that I hadn't been followed or else he wouldn't help me. I couldn't take it personal. That was how shit was.

Jimmy looked at me, a serious glare. The man loved me and I loved him too. He had three daughters and only one was in his life. The other two were distant in miles and spirit. The old man wanted a son and his older daughters felt the lack of love and interest he had in their lives. He regretted that time in his life. But regrets don't always bring our loved ones back.

"I found out that the son of Marco Chavez has him. And he's not returning him until he can recover the shipment he lost from the bust at LaGuardia several weeks back."

"How the fuck am I going to make that happen? That's gonna be impossible to do." I boomed. I knew it seemed like I had just screamed on Jimmy, but that wasn't my intention.

"I didn't make those demands. They came from him."

I didn't know what to say in response to Jimmy's last comment, so I buried my face in the palm of my hands. I tried to make sense of everything and hoped to come up with a solution but I couldn't so I looked up from my hands and expected that Jimmy would come up with an answer for me.

"Who in their right mind makes those type of demands? There's no fucking way that I'm gonna be able to get their shit back."

"I thought it was outlandish when I heard it. But hey, you asked me to find out and that's what I was told."

"So, what happens if I don't deliver?"

"Are you sure you're ready to hear this?"

"Do I have a choice?"

"Yeah, you do." Jimmy responded nonchalantly.

I took a deep breath and stuck my chest out a little bit. I had to show Jimmy that no matter what he was about to tell me, I could handle it. "Give it to me." I finally told him.

"You're gonna bury your brother-in-law if you don't. I even heard some talk about his parents coming up missing next. Not sure if that's accurate. But I do know that this Chavez guy is trying to make a name for himself, so he's gonna do whatever it takes to put the fear in men's hearts among these parts."

"Ahh man, I've gotta let Foxx know that he and his wife may be the next target." I uttered, thinking about the possibility of them getting snatched up by Miguel and some of the members of his organization.

"Whatever you do, never mention my name." Jimmy advised me and I immediately knew what that meant. Jimmy never wanted to be linked to anyone. If he fell, he was the type of man that would fall alone.

"Jimmy man, trust me, no one even knows that I know you. So, you wouldn't ever have to worry about me mentioning your name to anyone."

"Very good." He commented and then he grabbed a cigar from a wooden box on his desk. He held the cigar out for me to take but I told him no in a nonverbal gesture. "You know—Mr. Chavez really wants his shipment back. But he said he'll settle for it's street value." He concluded after he licked the cigar from top to bottom and stuck it into his mouth.

"And how much is that?"

"Five million." He replied after he lit his cigar.

"Five million!" I roared. Miguel Chavez was being pretty unreasonable. There was no fucking way

I'd be able to come up with that kind of money while the Feds are on our asses.

"Have you thought about the possibilities that you may have to walk away from this?" he asked and then he took a pull of the cigar.

Before I answered Jimmy I thought about whether he'd appreciate me being honest with him if I told him I had thought about turning my back on Reggie. I mean Reggie brought this shit on himself. I didn't ask for this war. He did. So, why am I taking all of the burden when he stayed here unprotected? Naomi and I begged him to leave with us but he refused. He was dead set on staying in New York. Now that decision has compromised his life. While I thought of an appropriate way to express my feelings to Jimmy without sounding like a fucking sell-out he broke the ice.

"Before you answer me, keep in mind that you're human first and a man second. I really don't care how you answer me. I just want you to bear in mind that either way you go will affect you."

I thought very hard about what Jimmy said. He was a very wise man. And he was right; whatever I decided to do concerning Reggie would definitely affect me. If I chose to turn my back on him, Naomi and her family wouldn't be able to forgive me. And if I chose to pay his ransom where would I get the money. There's got to be another way.

"Do the smart thing, drop your quest for your brother-in-law and get the hell out of town. Even if you came up with the dope or the money, you and I both know that Miguel isn't gonna let you and Reggie live. And if he got the chance to get the rest of Reggie's family, he's gonna make an example out of them too."

"Jimmy, I wished it was that easy." I said. I really didn't know what else to say. I thought for a minute. I had to process all of this. "Do you know where Miguel is keeping him and how many men Miguel has working for him."

"No, I don't know where he is being kept, but I do know that Reggie is being heavily guarded by at least ten to fifteen men. And getting to him isn't going to be easy with that type of manpower. So, here is something that'll help you along the way." He replied as he reached under his desk and handed me a medium-sized duffel bag. "There are weapons and cash in the bag. Enough paper for you to get it out of town and live comfortably for six months or a year, depending on your living expenses."

"You don't have to do this." I objected. I knew he was trying to pay me off but I didn't need his money. I needed a fucking miracle.

"Take it Damian. Trust me, it'll come in handy later."

I hesitated for a moment but then I took the bag. "Thanks Jimmy. You're a good man."

"I take care of those who take care of me," he replied.

I smiled,

"Stay alert." He warned me. And after I thanked him once again I made my exit.

During the drive back to the house, I thought about how Naomi would react after I told her that there was a chance that we wouldn't see Reggie again. I knew she wouldn't be able to handle that type of news. So I wondered if it would be wise to tell her anything. I guess I'd know when I crossed that bridge.

Jimmy told me some real shit today.

INTERNATIONALLY KNOWN:
NEW YORK'S FINEST (PART 2)

KIKI SWINSON

Naomi Waits for Damian to Return

Damian had been gone for a couple of hours now and I've gotten worried. He lied to me and assured me that as soon as he picked up one of those throwaway phones that he'd call me so I would have a number to contact him with. But he didn't keep his word.

I tried to watch TV while Damian was gone but my mind wouldn't allow me to concentrate on any of the shows that were on. I started to take a walk around the neighborhood but I knew if I walked out of that door in broad daylight then I'd been treading on thin ice. I couldn't compromise our true identity. We traveled too far for that.

While I paced the floors of the family room the doorbell rang. My heart skipped a beat because I knew it was Damian. I wasted no time running to open the door for him. I couldn't wait to jump into his arms. I knew seeing him would make all my worrying go away. It seemed like I couldn't get the door open fast enough and I was only a few feet away from the front door. "I'm coming," I yelled. And as soon as I unlocked the front door, I grabbed the doorknob and I opened it. To my surprise, the person at the front door wasn't Damian, it was a white man dressed as a fucking UPS delivery driver with a package in his hands. "Hi ma'am, I have a package for a Rita McKenzie." He said.

I stood there dumbfounded. I knew that there was no Rita McKenzie at this house, but for some reason I couldn't open my mouth to tell him. I was so caught off guard by his unexpected visit that I couldn't think straight. Not to mention, he looked like an undercover cop, so that had me on edge as well. "Would you like to sign for this package?" he asked me.

"I'm sorry but that person doesn't live here." I finally replied. I was nervous as hell. And I was waiting for him to pull out his badge and tell me that I was under arrest.

"Are you sure? Because this is an overnight package and it needs to be delivered." He pressed the issue.

"Yes, I'm sure. You have the wrong address."

"Okay, well thank you." He said and then he walked away.

I immediately shut the front door and locked it. I ran to the window and peeped through the window treatments to see where the UPS guy had walked off to and noticed him climbing back onto his truck. My heart raced uncontrollably because I knew deep down in my heart that this guy was working undercover. And I knew that it was a matter of time before he was going to send in the cavalry so I ran to the bedroom, grabbed my handbag and my luggage and headed for the back door. I had no idea where I was going but I knew that I had to get my ass out of this house.

Panic stricken, I ran out of the back door and stumbled down the back stairs. My heart rate sped up as I made my way away from the house. I didn't have any idea where I was going, all I knew was that I needed to get away from this house and do it fast. "Damian, where are you? Call me please." I uttered loud enough for only myself to hear.

There was an alley alongside of the house, so I took it. And when I got onto the next street I crossed over to the other side and entered into the nearby laundry mat. I was petrified being out here alone. Being in this laundry mat with these patrons staring at me only made me feel worse. There was an empty chair in the back of the facility so I marched straight to it with my luggage in hand and had a seat. I took a deep breath and tried to calm my nerves so I could figure out my next move. It was imperative for me to get in contact with Damian but since I had no way of doing so I pulled out my cell phone and called my father. The last meeting he and I had didn't end on a good note but I didn't let that deter me from calling him. He needed to know what was going on and then maybe he'd be able to help me figure out a way to get in contact with Damian before he had a chance to get back to the house. My worse fear was to lose him so hopefully we'd be able to get to him before they did.

"Daddy," I whispered.

"What's wrong baby? Why are you whispering? Are you okay?" my father asked me.

"No, I need you to come get me." I continued to whisper.

"What's the matter?"

"A white man dressed up like a UPS driver came to the house trying to get me to sign for a package for some lady named Rita Mckenzie and when I told him that he had the wrong address, he left. But I swear to you daddy, he looked just like a Narc."

"And where are you?"

"I   'm at the laundry mat two blocks away from the house.

"Where is Damian?" my father's questions continued.

"He went to see a friend. Daddy please hurry up and come get me."

"Which laundry mat is it?"

"I don't know daddy. Just come get me please." I replied frantically. But I spoke in a very low pitch. I couldn't let anyone in the laundry mat know what was going on. As far as I knew, everyone around me was suspect and I didn't trust them.

"Which way did you go when you left the house?" My father wanted to know.

"I left out the back door and ran in the opposite direction of the house."

"Okay. I know where you are. Just stay put and I'll be there in a minute."

"Daddy, I need you to try to get in touch with Damian before he goes back to the house. I will bet money that they're getting geared up right now to bust in there."

"Who knows that you're here beside me?"

"No one daddy. I haven't talked to anyone but you and Damian."

"Think maybe his contact turned over on you guys?"

"Daddy, I don't know anything about that guy he went to see. All I know is that his name is Jimmy. That's it."

"Well Chica, you stay put and I'll be there in a few minutes."

"Okay."

INTERNATIONALLY KNOWN: NEW YORK'S FINEST (PART 2)

KIKI SWINSON

Damian's Plan

Getting Reggie back wasn't going to be an easy task. But I was motivated to come up with a plan. I cruised slowly up the block where Naomi and I stayed and noticed that something wasn't right about the house. I started to stop the car but my intuition told me to keep driving after I noticed that the front door of the house was slightly ajar. It looked as if someone went inside, robbed it and left without closing the door behind them. I couldn't tell you if this was the case, but I did know that it didn't look right so I kept moving.

When I got to the next block, I made a left turn because it was a one-way street. I fought with the decision to turn back around but I knew I would be compromising myself. Then I thought about what if Naomi was inside of the house hurt and needed help? How could I help her if I bailed out and kept moving? But then I thought about the possibility of her being dead. The thought alone was unbearable but Jimmy did make me painfully aware that there was a good possibility that if Miguel didn't get his money he was going to kill Reggie and then he'd kill his family next.

I couldn't imagine losing Naomi. She was a part of my life now and I had vowed to protect her. So, that's what I intended to do.

After I made the left turn down the one-way street, I made another left turn on the next block. I figured I'd have a better chance of finding out who was in the house if I parked the car and traveled on foot and went in through the back. So after I pulled onto the next block I managed to find a parking space and ditched the car. All I could think about was finding Naomi alive. I swear, if anyone had hurt her, I was going to make them pay.

My adrenaline was pumping like crazy. I had been in a lot of situations where I had no idea how the outcome would turn out. Thinking back on those times, I was pretty nervous. But today, I was in a different mindset. Now I didn't care. I was prepared for whatever or whoever. I had my Glock with me and that's all I needed. If it meant I was about to take my last breath, then so be it. I was a man. And I had to be a man of my word.

I crossed the street on foot. Although I wore sunshades I still walked with my head down. I couldn't take any chances of anyone seeing my face. But surprisingly, someone did.

"Damian," I heard a woman say. It sounded like Naomi, so I turned around. Across the street waving me down was indeed Naomi. And Foxx stood next to her. I raced back across the street to greet them. I grabbed Naomi into my arms as soon as I got within a few feet of her.

"Come here, girl, I thought something happened to you," I said as I lifted her off the ground.

Foxx interrupted our brief reunion. "I take it you saw the front door cracked?"

I put Naomi down. "Yeah, I did. What's up with that?" I asked. I needed some answers.

"Naomi will explain everything to you because we gotta get out of here. So wait until I pull out and then you follow me," Foxx instructed us.

I escorted Naomi to my car while Foxx got into his. And just as he said, I waited for him to pull out into the road and when he finally did, I swerved into the road behind him. I was focused on staying on Foxx's tail, but I was also curious to find out what was going on.

"What the fuck is going on?" I asked Naomi.

"A white UPS driver looking just like a Narc told me he was delivering a package for a Rita McKenzie and asked me if I would sign for it. I told him he had the wrong address and after he left I got scared and ran out the back door."

"Did you leave the front door open?"

"No, I didn't. But after I left I called daddy and told him to try to get in contact with you so you wouldn't go back to the house. And when he showed up he told me that he stopped by the house and cracked the door open, because if you saw it, he knew you wouldn't go inside.

"So, you think the cops tried to deliver a package to the house?"

"Damian, I swear I am not crazy. I know what I saw and that guy looked just like a fucking cop. So I got out of there as fast as I could."

"Well, where are we going now?"

"We're going across town. My dad is taking us to another one of Stone's spots in Hackensack. He said we could hide out there as long as we're here."

"Did you get my bag from the house?"

"No, but my dad got it when he went there. He's got it in the car with him."

"A'ight," I replied and then I let out a long sigh.

Following Foxx through the streets of New Jersey was like traveling through a maze. It felt like we were going nowhere fast. I knew I shouldn't be driving around in broad daylight. This was definitely not a good look and I expressed it to Naomi.

"How far is this place? I'm ready to get there so we can put our heads together so we can get Reggie back." I said.

"I'm ready to get there too," she commented. I could tell she was irritated but she was more afraid than anything. So I held my head up like only a gangster would. I had to make her see how strong I was and that I would make everything that was wrong, right. And after everything was all said and done, I was going to come out looking like a real hero. "When you had that meeting with that guy Jimmy, did you tell him where we were hiding out?" she blurted out. That question came out of thin air.

"Hell nah! Why you ask me that?"

"Because me and my daddy were trying to figure out who else knew where we were."

"Nah, Naomi, me and Jimmy didn't talk about where I was at. The question never came up. He was more concerned about me bringing the heat to him. And besides, even if he knew, he ain't that type of cat. Jimmy is more thorough than that nigga Stone was. He's from the old school. And loyalty is all he got."

"Was he able to find out any information about Reggie?"

I hesitated before I answered Naomi. It was important that I say the right words to her. She was already in an uproar about the UPS driver so I knew I needed to tread lightly.

"Yeah, he found out who had Reggie," I finally replied.

"Is he still alive?"

"As far as we know."

"Who has him?"

"Miguel."

"Is there a ransom?"

"Yes."

"How much?"

"I was told that we could either get his shipment back or come up with five million cash."

"What happens if we don't?"

"Come on, Naomi, don't make me spell it out. You already know what we're dealing with. Miguel is a fucking lunatic. And he ain't gonna make shit easy for us."

INTERNATIONALLY KNOWN

"Oh my God! This is going to break my mother's heart when she finds out how much Reggie's ransom is. And my dad is going to fucking flip out." Naomi's voice was cracking. I could tell she was on the verge of tears. Knowing that your brother has been kidnapped and was being held for a multi-million dollar ransom can be heartbreaking. I was sure she felt in her heart that she wasn't going to ever see him again.

"Why don't you hold out on telling your mother?" I suggested.

"What about my dad? You wanna keep this from him too?"

"Of course not. As soon as we get to our destination, I'm gonna tell him everything I know.

"He's not gonna be too happy about the five million dollar ransom."

"He's trying to make a come back from the bust."

Naomi sucked her teeth. "He's a fucking asshole! You knew Reggie and I didn't have any control over that shit!"

"Naomi, you know niggas don't care about who's fault it is. And they don't give a fuck how rich you made them either. At the end of the day it's business."

"Well, have you figured out how we're gonna come up with all that damn money?"

"I've thought of a few ways but I'm gonna have to run them by Foxx first."

"You do that." she commented nonchalantly and then she turned her focus back out the passenger side window.

We rode in silence the rest of the way to our new safe house. The new house was just as nice as the old safe house. One thing I had to say about Stone, the man had very good taste. This was a brick house, two-story and very spacious.

We sat in the living room and chilled out after taking a quick tour around the entire house. Primarily to make sure someone wasn't hiding out in a closet or under a bed or something. We were still paranoid about what had just happened. We had to be extra cautious, so a little paranoia was good for the soul in this case . . . or good enough to keep us alive. *So I hoped.*

INTERNATIONALLY KNOWN:
NEW YORK'S FINEST (PART 2)

KIKI SWINSON

Naomi's Strategy

I know I was being short with Damian but I'm just one big ball of emotions. I don't know if I'm coming or going as I sat around and waited for the meeting to start. My father got a phone call while Damian and I were getting more acquainted with our new house, so he excused himself to deal with the caller. Damian asked me if I was okay a few times too many. I knew he meant well but now wasn't the time to ask me such a dumb question. What possessed him to ask me if I was all right when I was dealing with the possibility that my only brother could be dead? In addition to that, I had just had an encounter with a cracker who could have been the fucking police. And if I hadn't acted as quickly as I had, I'd probably be in federal custody right now. The thought of being in the hands of the fucking police while my brother was out here fighting for his life didn't sit well me with me at all. Damian had better come up with a plan because if he doesn't act fast and help get Reggie back then I don't think that he and I will make it to the next faze in our relationship. In fact, it would be over.

Finally after sitting around for more than ten minutes, my father joined us. I sat there and listened intensely as Damian told my father and me about what Jimmy had said. The more information I heard, the more pissed off I got. For Miguel this was war. He was out to make a name for himself and he wanted to use Reggie, Damian and me to make his name. Listening to Damian run everything down to us, I was sure we were all going to end up in coffins. My parents would be burying us side by side, I was sure of that.

Once Damian completed filling us in on him and Jimmy's conversation, I was surprised when my father said he had just spoken with Miguel. My heart dropped into the pit of my stomach. I didn't know whether to ask my father what they talked about or curse him out for not telling us he had that asshole on the phone. My mind raced from point A to point B in two seconds flat. Thankfully my father derailed my plans by speaking first. God knows how he would've reacted if I disrespected him. "Damian, I don't know where Jimmy got his information from, but he was pretty damn accurate," my father stated. "Miguel Chavez wants his dope back or we have to replace it with five million cash. He said that the five million dollars is what he would've made from the streets if we would've delivered his product safely to him."

"Daddy please tell me why you didn't tell us you were talking to him on the phone?" I blurted out. I couldn't keep my mouth closed very long. I was visibly upset. I needed to know why my dad left us in the dark. I would've given anything to speak to that motherfucker. I definitely had a lot to say to him.

"Because I knew you would not have handled it well. You would've let your emotions get the best of you if I would've told you he was on the phone. He knows we want to get Reggie back so in situations like this, you can't show any weakness. You gotta be firm and let the other person involved know that it's about business and nothing else." My father explained.

"Well, did you tell him that we didn't have that kind of money?" I asked. I was stressed the hell out and he sensed it. This whole fucking situation was crazy if you asked me and I truly wanted to hurt somebody and that somebody was a bastard named Miguel Chavez.

"Of course, I told him we didn't have that kind of money. I also told him that it would take us months to come to get that kind of money, if we could get it at all. He told me we had exactly one week, seven days."

"Are you fucking serious? Seven fucking days! That's it?" Damian facetiously asked.

"Yep, seven whole days," my father repeated.

"That's not enough time Foxx. We're just fooling ourselves to think we'll be able to come up with that money in that short period of time." Damian continued.

"Why don't you get back on the phone with him and ask for a few more days." I chimed in. I felt like I had to put the heat underneath my father's ass. Whether they knew it or not, I knew how Marco and his son Miguel operated. I used to fuck Marco on a regular basis. He was my sugar daddy so that gave me more insight on how far we'd be able to push him.

"I don't think that'll be necessary." My father said flatly.

"And why not? He knows he's being unreasonable. All you've gotta do is press him hard enough, he'll give him."

"I've tried it already. He won't budge."

I stood up from the chair and held out my hand. "Give me your phone and let me talk to him. He'll listen to me." I pressed on.

"Naomi, baby, I can't let you get in the middle. So, will you just let me and Damian handle it our way?" my father begged.

"I'm already in the middle. It was my people at the airport that allowed Miguel's shipment to be compromised in the first place."

"While I understand that honey, the rules have changed and Miguel is not as friendly as you remember him to be."

"Daddy please don't patronize me." I said and then I sighed. "All I'm saying is that, if you let me talk to him, I'm sure he'll give us more leverage."

"Look Naomi, I know you mean well, but I can't let you put yourself out there like that. Just let me and Damian handle everything from here and if we need your help, we'll let you know." My father replied. He made it plain and simple that this was a mission that he and Damian were going to handle their own way. And no matter how much I whined, bitched or moaned, he wasn't going to let me do things my way. So, I threw in the towel and asked him to explain to me how they planned to get Reggie back. "Well daddy, since you

INTERNATIONALLY KNOWN

wanna do this what's your plan?" I asked. I knew he
had thought about a solution. Somewhere in that mind
of wisdom, I knew he had thought this whole thing
out. So, I was ready to do whatever was necessary.

"Truthfully, Chica, I'm not sure," he said weakly. "I have access to Stone's money and I can get my
hands on a couple of mill, and your mother and I have
another three hundred and fifty grand we can get a
hold of, but that still leaves us two point six five mill
in the hold."

"Well, Jimmy just gave me two hundred grand,"
Damian added.

"What about the offshore accounts your brother
set up for you and him?" my father asked me.

"Reggie cleaned those out after all of this shit
began," I added. "Damian and I were able to get a
hundred grand out before Reggie cleaned it all out.
But we only have about seventy-five left."

"Okay, that gives us two million six hundred
twenty-five thousand dollars," my father stated. "Now
we only need two million three hundred seventy-five
thousand."

"I know what we can do," I just blurted out. I
don't know why I hadn't thought about this sooner. It
was genius. It was now just a point of getting the
words to come out of my mouth in a convincing way.
"Remember, how we were getting hit . . . you know,
motherfuckers robbing us and shit."

"Yeah," Damian said.

"Well, we'll just do the same shit to the mother-fuckers who's rocking the streets now. They wouldn't know what hit them if we plan this shit right."

I looked at both Damian and my father and both were thinking. I was patient. Although I wanted them to like my idea, I was cool and calm. I knew they both had to let my plan to be a stick-up kid marinate before they just came out and accepted it . . . after all, I was talking about some dangerous shit.

"Nah, that shit takes too much planning. Not to mention, it can be a deathtrap if shit don't go as planned. And besides that, I can't go out there alone and stick my neck out there like that." Damian object-ed.

"You won't be doing it alone," I added. "This is a Bonney and Clyde operation."

"Oh, hell nah, Naomi, I wouldn't dare let you get involved in some fucked up shit like this!" Damian objected furiously.

"Bullshit, Damian, Reggie is my brother and if I have to rob and kill some bitch ass niggas, then so be it!" I let my voice be heard loud and clear.

"Foxx, tell your daughter to stand down!"

We both looked at my father and then he sur-prised the hell out of me. "You know what Damian, I actually think Naomi may have something here," he said. "Think about it, no one will expect for a woman to rob them. The drug boys running shit out there are happy with their territories. Everything is good. And since Reggie's operation was shut down, everybody is making what they consider to be their piece of the pie.

INTERNATIONALLY KNOWN

In other words, everybody's guard is down, and this may be the best time to ruffle their feathers and take them out of their comfort zone."

"Foxx, seriously?" Damian asked with shock on his face.

"I'm very serious," Foxx replied.

"But Foxx, we are talking about some shit that needs to be planned accordingly. Not to mention, we need to do a week's worth of surveillance just to make sure we doing this shit right. And then on top of that, we're gonna need a couple of getaway cars."

"Don't worry about that, I'll be able to get my hands on four or five different cars. Just tell me when and where you're gonna need them," my father rebutted. And then he turned his focus back on me. He looked me squarely in the eyes and said, "Do you think you can do this, baby girl? This is definitely a grown man's game and if something goes wrong, you or Damian could lose your life in a second. Now I could have already possibly lost one son, I don't want to lose my daughter too."

"I can do this dad," I said with confidence. I hoped he heard the seriousness in my voice and accepted those words as strength. Reggie was my brother and no fucking way was I sitting on the sidelines and just chilling while shit was going down. I was my brother's keeper.

"Are you two fucking crazy? I mean come on Foxx, you can't be serious about all of this." Damian continued to object.

"Enough of the shit, Damian," I retorted. "Either you are in or you're not. But make a decision, because I be damned if I'm going to allow Miguel to kill Reggie without us at least trying." I looked at Damian and I could still see the trepidation on his face. Damian was a soldier and he wasn't afraid. I knew the deal. And quiet as kept, my father knew what was up as well. He was worried about me and didn't want me to be in the middle of some crazy ass shit like this.

Damian didn't say anything but his eyes said a lot. I knew he wished he could just pull me to the side and talk to me, but he knew I wouldn't listen. He also knew that I would tell him to go fuck himself. I'm sure he was worried about me in the long run, calling off the relationship. But he also needed to know that family came first and if he wasn't down with how I wanted things to be handled, he definitely had a reason to be worried. In this case, family over shadowed love.

"Let's talk it out first and see how we can came to a bulletproof plan," my father intervened before Damian and I went at it. He was right. Maybe if we talked it out, we could resolve this shit.

"Yeah, I'm down for that," Damian said weakly.

"Check this out, Damian I know for a fact there's two different operations in Harlem, the same in the Bronx as well as three separate operations in Queens and a couple of others here in Jersey. That's at least nine separate operations we could hit up. Who knows if we don't waste any time we could probably do surveillance on all of those spots within a couple of days.

INTERNATIONALLY KNOWN

We could park all the different cars from a distance or we could get on the rooftops of the buildings with binoculars. I know if we sit on the rooftops we'll be able to see everything we need to see." My father explained.

"Come Foxx, nine operations in two days in all parts of the city and Jersey too is a helluva lot, you know that." Damian complained.

"Yeah, it's a lot," my father agreed. "But when it comes to the surveillance, I'm gonna get in on the action. I won't let you and my baby girl, do all the legwork. I want Reggie back as much you guys do so it's not an option for me to sit this one out. I will be at every site, that way there will be no fuck ups."

I wanted to be pissed at Damian for doubting my father but I knew we needed to keep the drama to a minimum. I had to be cool and hear him out because I wanted us to do this shit right. Not only that, I didn't want to die nor did I want him to die or my father for that matter so that meant that we had to be there for one another and listen to what the next person had to say.

"Look, I just want to get this over with. Remember Miguel said we only had a week and the clock is ticking as we speak." I chimed in.

"Chica, I know you're anxious. And I know the clock is ticking but we've got to establish the rules of engagement and assign everyone's role." My father expressed.

I sat back once again and took the backseat. I decided that it would be in everyone's best interest to let him do the talking this time around. And after my father gave everyone's their assignment we stopped to mull over how everything would turn out. I had no doubts whatsoever. I just wanted to get the ball rolling before we ran out of time. Damian had a few questions, though.

"So you're saying that one of us will be in a car and the remaining two will pick the locations on different rooftops so we'd be able to check out the same location at the same time?" Damian asked.

"Yes, that's exactly what I'm saying." My father said.

"Come on Foxx, let's be real. It's not gonna be that easy. Those young cats out there in Harlem are fucking scavengers and they're living by their own rules. So if we show up to their building acting like we belong there so we can get to the roof, we're gonna get stopped right at the front door."

"Those guys aren't that smart. And they're not as organized as y'all were."

"Daddy, we been robbed before." I blurted out. Our operation wasn't that rock solid and I had to remind my father of that.

"The only reason that happened was because you guys got hit by your own workers. No one else would've been able to penetrate your spots even if they tried." My father expressed.

My father definitely had a lot of confidence in us. He must've seen something in us that we didn't see ourselves. I felt like either way, the job has to be done for the sake of my brother Reggie.

INTERNATIONALLY KNOWN

"I sure wished that Stone was here. I know he would've handled everything."

I could tell Foxx still missed his best friends. Whenever the subject of Stone had come up, it was as if he refused to let the man go. Not only that, it was apparent that he didn't want to accept that Stone was dead. I definitely understood where he was coming from. Shit, I didn't want to accept that Reggie had gotten himself in such a fucked up situation.

"You know what, Foxx?" Damian said. "We may be able to pull this shit off if the element of surprise is on our side. And if the same underlings are in the business that was there when we ran shit and they have moved up, then we could possibly do this."

I didn't say anything. Inside, my heart was jumping up and down. I was glad Damian was finally coming to his senses. Now I knew I knew the writing wasn't quite scribbled on the wall yet, but we were more than halfway there.

"We can do this," Foxx guaranteed us. "We just need to do our planning now and I say we start this shit now. Let me jump on the phone and get us some getaway cars lined up. Plus, I need to go back to the house in Teaneck and see if everything is all right. If so, I need to get the guns and ammo that Stone kept in the house."

"Did he keep shit here too?" I asked.

"Yes he did," he smiled. I think it was a smile of remembering his friend and how obsessive the man was with being prepared for any and everything.

"I really think this can work," I said. Damian and Foxx looked at me once again. But I didn't care. I felt good about this. And the fact that Damian forced half-ass smirk on his face, gave me even more hope. It was a start.

"You good with a firearm?" he asked me.

"I'm very good with a gun," I answered. "It's time for me to step up as well. I could probably out-shoot you."

"That may be true, but have you ever shot any-one before."

It was a good question and my mind went back to my dream of rescuing Reggie. I thought about it, could I really be a warrior bitch if I had to be? The more I thought about it, the more I realized I could. If my brother's life depended on it, which it did, then I could do it.

"Yeah, Damian, when it comes to killing to pro-tect those I love, I can do this," I replied with confidence. "You know why?"

"Why?"

"Because you remember that day you saved my ass in the parking garage of the mall?"

"Yeah."

"That was some heroic shit you did. I knew then that what you did Damian, you done out of love. I knew then that my brother's best friend had sacrificed his life for his best friend's sister's life. You stepped up, Damian and you didn't have to."

"Oh, no I had to play the bodyguard back then. Reggie would've had my head on a platter if I hadn't done what I did."

"Well in any case, I wanna thank you."

"Naomi, you don't have to thank me. I did that out of respect and loyalty to your bother and your father. So, there's really nothing else to be said about it."

"Well, just let me say that that particular day you showed me that I could count on you in any situation. Believe me Damian you stole my heart. And I also know that what you are doing now is because of the loyalty you have for my brother. So, thank you."

"Don't thank me. Just listen to me a little more. Show me that you trust me to make all the major decisions and that you'll trust me when I tell you that I wouldn't ever hurt you.

I said nothing. But I did nod my head. I even smiled at him a couple of seconds later, so he'd know that I was down for him one hundred percent.

It was obvious that he loved me and I also knew he loved Reggie, but this was about us. The feelings he had for me. Those same feelings he extended to my family in the name of love. And I was down for that.

Damian has another side to him after all.

INTERNATIONALLY KNOWN:
NEW YORK'S FINEST (PART 2)

KIKI SWINSON

Damian the Criminal

We had already scoped out three places and were on spot number four. It was the same job for each of us at every spot. Foxx was in the car while Naomi and I were on the rooftop of separate buildings. The thing that made our plan run smoothly was that Foxx put a small investment in some good ass long lens, long range digital cameras. This was definitely the way to go. I say to hell with trying to remember anything or write shit down, we had it on digital memory.

As a rule, I suggested we still write some of our intell down that we may miss on camera. The only bad thing was we hadn't programmed the cameras for day and time. That was something we still needed to do. But all and all, we were on our way.

We were in Queens at a four-plex of buildings called the Butler Sky Rise. They were numbered one through four and I knew them well. Everyone familiar with the four-plex, called them by their initials, BSR. I used to fuck with a half-black & half-Filipino chick in BSR #3. Even today, I would rank her number one, regardless of how much I loved Naomi. That chick definitely knew how to threw her pussy at me. She used to fuck my brains out and gave me head like it would be the last time her mouth would touch a dick and like I was on death row, never to have my dick sucked again. The only reason I left that bitch alone was because she got hooked on heroin. Heroin was deadly and it could turn the most beautiful woman in the world to the ugliest bitch alive.

Quiet as it was kept, I would love to get that pussy again. I laughed to myself. That was the biggest lie in the world. I wasn't available plus I wasn't on the block anymore. Naomi was my life now and as much as I wanted other chicks, or I should say, new pussy, my days of philandering around were over with for now. I was like most pussy whipped niggas today, I looked at other pussy and wondered what it would be like to taste that shit or stick my dick in between those hot legs. But that was wishful thinking and I didn't let that shit bother me. Shit, I had prime Grade A pussy at home and there was no way I was fucking that up. Too many niggas threw away good pussy for stupid ass chicks that aren't worth a damn and I didn't want to be a part of that club. Fuck that!

The Butler Sky Rise buildings were ran by a nigga who went by D.D. Unfortunately, I knew that nigga all too well. He used to kick my ass when we were younger. I should say when I was young. I don't think that motherfucker was ever young. I was eight or nine when he was fifteen or sixteen, kicking my ass like I was his age or something. So I owed his black ass.

D.D. was short for Devil Daniels. What kind of fucked up shit was that? I knew personally his real name was Dante Daniels and I wanted to fuck his ass up really bad. He was still a bitch ass nigga running over top of the young cats in his crew.

Foxx had dug deep into Stone's arsenal of weapons and found what he really wanted. Taser guns with power up to twenty-five thousand volts. Shit that would knock motherfuckers completely out and then some. That many volts would shut a nigga's system down for days and weeks on end. That is, if it hadn't killed the nigga first.

I couldn't wait to shoot a few volts through that bitch ass nigga, Dante. Fuck that nigga D.D! And as soon as I get the chance, all hell will break loose. I laughed at the thought of making that nigga pay for what he did to me back when I was a kid. Karma was definitely a bitch!

I was impressed with Foxx. That old man had skills. He supplied me and Naomi with some heavy artillery. The shit he had for us could be used to take out a small army. We were both strapped with two Taser guns and two handguns, which included four clips with nine bullets in each clip, and of all things, flash bang grenades. And to top it off, we had our cameras, which was simply amazing. Hell, I could see shit in the next county with this powerful ass camera.

The weapons for now were for protection. Just in case something happened. But I was convinced we could do some shit now. As in, right now. The more I thought about it, the more I wanted to take down Dante now. I wanted that motherfucker to know that he was never a fucking Devil Daniels, but just good old, lame ass Dante Daniels.

Then I saw the man himself fucking up as usual. He was in Butler Sky Rise #1 on the twelfth floor of the fifteenth floor building. But that wasn't it. What convinced me to do a little mission of my own was when I zoomed my camera to BSR #4, on the third floor and saw Dante's bitch, Rita, going in the floor safe of their apartment. What fucked me up was Rita went in the safe and didn't spin the dial to the combination lock safe, she just opened it and closed it right back up.

Now as soon as I took my eyes off Rtia, I turned my focus and zoomed back to BSR #1, where Dante was eating the hell out of some other bitch's pussy. His fat ass was completely naked and he was putting in overtime with this chick. From where I was posted up, homegirl didn't look half bad. I could tell she had a phat ass even though she was lying on her back. I could also see how deflated her titties were too. I was a breast and ass man, so she didn't fit the bill for me. But when you're a fat, slob like Dante, you had to take what you could get.

"Oh, shit," I said.

"What's up?" Foxx said in my earpiece. Yeah, Foxx had also bought us some throwaway phones with Bluetooth technology. He and Naomi and I were on a third-way call. So we'd make voice notes to each other on interesting shit we saw.

"Yeah, something good," Naomi joined in.

"Yeah," I replied. "We are about to get real up in this motherfucker. Naomi, I'm looking at D.D. while he's fucking some chick in BSR #1, and his girl Rita is in his spot in BSR #4 with their son and check it out." I stopped my thought as I zoomed the camera in on Rita's place.

"Damian, what's going on?" Naomi asked.

"This shit is perfect," I responded. "We are about to rob this motherfucker's crib while he is BSR #1 eating some other chick's pussy."

"I don't think that's a good idea, Damian," Foxx chimed in. "Everybody knows D.D. keeps four armed soldiers outside his joint at all times."

"I agree with Foxx," Naomi said.

"Nah, we are doing this shit," I reiterated. "Foxx, this shit is crazy but classic. Rita opened and closed a floor safe without spinning a dial or keying in a code in a keypad. This shit is just wide open . . . open and close and that's it. And on top of that, guess what?"

"What?" Naomi was anxious to know.

"Two of his soldiers just stepped inside of his apartment. And wait, I think something is about to go down." I said and then I fell silent trying to gather more information.

"What are they doing?" Foxx wanted to know.

"Yeah, what's going on?" Naomi asked.

"Both niggas are in that niggas bedroom with Rita backed into a corner." I finally spoke up as I continued to see what was going on.

"What are they doing to her?" Naomi continued to question me.

"Oh my God! Those niggas are about to run a train on her."

"You're lying." Naomi said.

"Yeah, Damian, stop pulling our legs."

"Foxx, I'm telling you some real shit right now. Those niggas are getting it in right now. That ho just pulled their pants down and is actually sucking both of their dicks right now."

"No shit," Foxx said.

"No shit. Foxx, this is what we are going to do. Give Naomi and me ten minutes to get to the building. This shit needs to be synchronized. Naomi, we are going to use one of your flash bang grenades if we have to, but I don't think it will come to that. I want you to get your taser out and go to the other side of the building, between BSR 3 and 4, and enter that way. Take the elevator up if you can."

"I see where you're going with this. I take it you want me to take out the clown on the other end of the hallway as soon as I get off the elevator, and then you are going to surprise the asshole probably guarding the door, right?" Naomi confirmed her position.

"Yeah, that's it."

"Got it."

"Naomi, I need you to hit him with everything you have. You know all of D.D's guys live on that floor. So if you hit old boy with all the Taser juice, that motherfucker won't be able to scream or anything. And I plan on doing the same. Then don't run down the hallway, because somebody may hear you. Walk as fast as you can without running."

"Damian, let's do this!"
And with that, it was on.

INTERNATIONALLY KNOWN

INTERNATIONALLY KNOWN:
NEW YORK'S FINEST (PART 2)

KIKI SWINSON

I'm Naomi the Bitch

The thought of being one step closer to getting my brother back gave me somewhat of an adrenaline booster. It felt like I was riding on a fast train leaving the station and I was the conductor. I knew Damian couldn't stand D.D., but this was business and more important, this was a good opportunity to make a big score. And even though we were being a little hasty by taking on this job quicker than expected, I believed that things would work out if we stayed focused.

I was on a rooftop a couple of streets parallel to the Butler Sky Rises. I had to haul ass to get where I needed to be in ten minutes. It was the same for Damian. We had to beat the street if we wanted to get this shit started. I couldn't believe we were actually about to commit a heist. But what was really unbelievable was how excited I had become. I was really amped up.

I relayed to Foxx and Damian that I had made it to the building. And after I entered into the building I headed directly towards the elevator and I was greeted by one of D.D.'s men who was guarding the elevator. I recognized the procedure. It was the same routine

Reggie used to employ when we ran our operation so I didn't waste time with what I came to do. And before he could blink his eyes good enough, I pulled out my Glock 27, pointed it in the young motherfucker's face and told him to get his ass on the elevator. Thank God no one else was in the hallway.

Instead of doing as I instructed him this young ass nigga laughed at me. I swear I couldn't believe my eyes. And as he was about to say something I push my gun in his mouth and busted up his lip. It also sounded like I knocked a tooth or two out.

"Give me your piece, you little bitch," I said.

"Bitch—"

"Shut up before I shoot your stupid ass," I stated. This young punk was my height and that made me feel good because I had a surprise for his ass.

After he finally got on the elevator I stood directly behind him, with my Glock pushed against his back. And as soon as the doors closed, I started pistol-whipping his young ass. He had pissed me the fuck off by disrespecting me. I couldn't tell you how many times I hit his ass in his face and head. But I knew the number was close to ten. And with the pistol whipping came my foot in his balls and face. I didn't know what had came over me. I figured I was flipping out on this guy because of the hurt I felt knowing that my brother could be going through the same harsh punishment. What I really wanted to do was inflict pain on Miguel. But I guessed this dumb ass nigga would do for now.

After I got tired of kicking and beating this wanna-be ass drug dealer, I put my piece away and pulled out the taser gun. I should have been nervous but I wasn't. All the while I was doing my thing, my earpiece was going crazy with Foxx and Damian in my ear wanting to know what was going on. So I finally told them we were on and I was about to step off the elevator. "Let's get this party started gentlemen." I said in a menacing way.

When the elevator doors opened, the nigga posted up on my side had his back towards me. I guess he thought I was one of his boys coming up. But he was about to be in for a rude awakening.

I crept to the edge of the elevator door and saw another one of Dante's boys standing at the front door of the apartment with his ear pressed against the door, listening to what was happening inside the apartment. My only cover was the scarf and cap on my head and sunshades I had on. I hope that concealed who I was.

Even before he could turn around, I hit the young boy with all twenty-five thousand volts and he was indeed out of it. As soon as his homeboy turned around, Damian came through the staircase door and did the same thing. These young boys were carrying AR-15 assault rifles and didn't have time to use them. I had intentions to use them so I wasted no time grabbing the one my guy had and hurriedly made my way to Damian.

The BSRs had ten apartments on each floor. D.D.'s apartment consisted of two apartments made into one. BSR was the top dog of apartments, as in three bedrooms per apartment versus the other buildings, which only had one or two bedrooms.

When I finally came within one foot of Damian he instantly kicked in the front door. He had already told me to stay at the door in case someone came or any one of the two woke up, which I seriously doubted.

When he kicked in the door, I couldn't believe my eyes. This slutty bitch was sucking on one of Dante's boy's dick while the other cat was fucking her from behind. This was porno shit at its best. Even more so since she was Hispanic and both of D.D.'s guys were black, and dogging the shit out of their boss's lady.

Before any one of them niggas could grab their piece, Damian hit one with his Taser and the other one just froze. I couldn't see Damian's face, but something told me he was smiling. He had on sunshades as well, but he was wearing an afro wig along with an O.J. Simpson mask. I thought that shit was funny.

"Why you standing there? Aren't you supposed to be trained to go?" Damian asked the guy as he stood before us. I could see the fear in his eyes. This poor guy was scared. I'm sure Dante would be very disappointed if he knew this nigga he recruited hadn't had any heart. I knew he would not have made it in our operation. No way.

After Damian realized this punk ass nigga wasn't going to respond to his question, he smacked him upside the head with his Glock 40 and he instantly was knocked the fuck out. I literally stood there like I was

INTERNATIONALLY KNOWN

watching a movie. Damian was on some Bonny and Clyde shit for real.

Immediately after he knocked the other guy out, he grabbed D.D.'s bitch by her blonde locks, dragged her into the bedroom and pushed her down to the floor. She watched in mere shock as Damian pulled the rug aside and opened a door hatch in the floor. After he opened the safe, he grabbed a pillow off the bed and took the pillowcase and put the money in the pillowcase.

"I'll be right back," he told me and then he disappeared. I didn't know what was up.

"Please don't kill me." She began to plead for her life. I wanted to be sympathetic, but somehow I blocked out all of my emotions. All I was concerned about was my brother. And if it meant that we had to rob her and kill her to get one step closer to bringing Reggie home, then she was going to be one dead bitch.

Moments later, Damian reappeared. But he had a fucking kid in his arm. He was a cute little guy and he had this chick's features so there was no denying that he was her son. "Please don't hurt my son, I would do anything if you'll just leave him out of this." she cried.

"Shut the fuck up bitch!" Damian roared.

"What are you doing?" I asked. I was somewhat confused by this sudden move on his part.

"We are going to make some money off this lil cat," Damian said. I could tell by his voice he was full of adrenaline.

I didn't say one word, now it was time to get the fuck out of here. I felt that if something needed to be said then it could be said later. In reality, things happened for a reason. Relatively speaking, it was what it was. We were definitely criminals now.

We made our way down the staircase and came out on the end of the building into the parking lot of BSR #4. Thankfully my father had just driven up so we jumped in and then he sped off. Damian was in the back seat with the kid. The little guy gave Damian a run for his money. He kicked and screamed the entire time Damian transported him to the car. I watched in amazement during their exchange. I gave the kid his props, he put up a big fight before Damian got tired and smacked his butt a couple of times and told him to shut the hell up and stop acting a fool before he killed him. I knew it was just an idle threat especially after I looked at Damian and he smiled at me. This tactic of Damian showed me how far a person would go to get shit done in an orderly fashion. Too bad the little boy became a pawn in our scheme.

From what I gathered when Damian spoke of Dante', it became apparent that shit was about to hit the fan. Damian expressed how Dante' would take the news of his son getting kidnapped. "I would pay anything to see that niggas face after his girl tells him we got his their son," Damian commented.

"I know you left her alive for a reason, but I think she's going to cause more harm than good." I told him.

INTERNATIONALLY KNOWN

Damian smiled. "No, she's going to do exactly what she was instructed to do."

I let out a long sigh. "If you say so," I commented and then I left the subject alone. Whatever plan Damian had brewing inside his brain had better be a good one. If it were up to me, I would've done the heist and kept it moving. We didn't need to kidnapped this little boy because all he was going to do was slow us down. And time was something we didn't have. But then again, if Damian felt taking him would give us a pot of gold at the end of the rainbow then let the chips fall where they may.

After the little boy resisting I looked at him and thought about how I'd feel if someone took my son. And for the first, time I was able to show a little empathy. It would break my fucking heart if someone ran up in my apartment and took my child. I would be a fucking basket case. And I'd admit myself into a psycho ward so I wouldn't have to deal with the pain. This shit we got ourselves in was serious and if one thing messed up then we'd all be in some serious shit.

"Don't get caught up in the hype. Remember we gotta to stay focused okay?" I reminded him. I knew Damain wanted Dante' as much as I wanted Miguel. I could see it in his eyes. To defeat Dante' at any cost would be a huge victory for Damian.

INTERNATIONALLY KNOWN:
NEW YORK'S FINEST (PART 2)

KIKI SWINSON

Damian's World

We were exhausted but we had one helluva night. We had done shit none of us thought we would have been doing at the beginning at the day. I honestly didn't know if we had stepped over the line or not. We had robbed niggas from the streets just to hand the money over to another street nigga. Now how fucked up was that? I knew it sounded wild. But that was just a way of life for us. We lived in a dog eat, dog world and everyone played by their own rules. In this case, we were forced to do things we never thought we'd do. Just a few months back, Reggie and I was bring in one to one million and a half dollars in revenue from our dope spots. But now we aren't making shit. We are robbing niggas and their spots for forty, fifty and sixty grand, which was chump changed when we were dealing. Who thought we'd have to stoop this low? I guess what they say is true, never say never.

Instead of going back to New Jersey, we decided to go back and hit the drug dealers we had already scoped out. Everything was smooth and unexpected. We were all over the damn city. Our goal was to hit as many spots as possible before anyone heard about the news of us hitting D.D. and his operation. Plus, we knew the news of the kidnapping would run rampant. It would actually fuck some niggas up and we had to do damage now, because we knew the criminal element would be ready for us.

Before we made our next stop I knocked the little boy unconscious, then I dumped all the money out of the pillowcase and used it to cover his head with it. "Don't you think that was just a little to harsh?" Naomi asked me.

"Come on baby, I didn't hurt him that bad. And besides, it was either knock him out or kill 'em." I commented and then I cracked a smile. I wanted her to lighten up. It wasn't the end of the world.

Once I got the pillowcase on his head, I laid him down on the backseat. "Foxx, I'm gonna need you to pay close attention to him while Naomi and I got into this next spot." I warned him.

"I'm on guard." He assured me. And then he smiled at me.

Keeping all of that in consideration, we decided to do something completely different. We went into the home of Pretty Boy Pedro. He was the biggest heroin dealer in the Bronx. And to keep this heist simple, Naomi and I did the same thing we did to Dante'. We kidnapped his three-year-old daughter. And believe me, it worked out great because Pedro, just like Dante, was occupied with something else. The only difference, Pedro was a very confident cat. No one in their right mind would fuck with his family. This nigga was so feared and respected that he didn't have bodyguards protecting them. Too bad, we didn't fall in that category of people. We were bandits and we handled things the way we wanted to.

At the end of the night Foxx shook his head at all the havoc we created. I understood his hesitancy in what we did. But in the midst of it all we were able to take over six hundred thousand dollars from the spots we robbed. The hit we did on Dante' resulted in over four hundred thousand dollars. And before we released both kids, were asked both men to release a half-million dollars each. If they weren't able to pay, then it was settled that they wouldn't be returned.

This was just day two of our seven day deadline. We had hoped to have collect at least two-thirds of the money we needed to get Reggie back.

It was five-thirty in the morning when we got in. We put both kids in the basement and Foxx volunteered to look after them. I was glad because I needed to sleep. Hell, we all needed sleep. And that's what we did.

I woke up at around ten-thirty that morning and the first thing I did was check on Foxx and the kids. Foxx was in the kitchen cooking breakfast. Although he had plenty of food out, he was presently just cooking for himself. "If I had known you'd be getting up, I would've cooked more food," he commented.

"It's cool. I really don't have any appetite anyway." I told him.

"After that all nighter we pulled last night you gotta put something on your stomach." He told me.

INTERNATIONALLY KNOWN

"Okay then, do what you do." I replied. He was right I needed to put something on my stomach.

"Thought about when it would be a good time to call those kids' people?" Foxx questioned me. He kept his back to me while he prepared his food over the stove.

"I plan to do it in the next thirty minutes. I just wanted to run a few things by you first before I made the calls."

"What's up?" Foxx asked.

"I was wondering would it be a good idea to have Naomi make the phone call?" I suggested. I was anxious and I wanted to kick everything in gear. Especially after the heist we pulled off last night. Naomi and I were in spontaneity mode, not planning mode. So now we needed to plan and move forward cautiously.

"No. That wouldn't be a good idea considering the type of cats we're dealing with. I think you should call them, make your demands and let everything play out." Foxx began. He was cooking eggs, for both of us now, not just himself. "You are the de facto leader of our little makeshift operation right now. But as a leader, you have to think and be prepared for leadership. Last night was an outstanding and profitable night for us. And it became very risky. So, do everyone a favor the next time around and start using your head."

"Okay. I can respect that." I replied. I knew Foxx wouldn't lie to me. He looked at me like I was his son. So whatever he told me, I knew it was for my best interest. In addition to pointing out the mistakes I made the night before, Foxx also dropped some knowledge on me. He pulled my card on some Albert Einstein shit. I was told as a child by my uncles to never assume an O.G. doesn't know what the fuck they're talking about because they are some wise cats. They change with the time and eight-five percent of them always kept it gangsta. But most importantly, they were loyal.

I continued to look at Foxx after he finished talking. Back in Memphis, Naomi told me some good things about him, but this was the first I was seeing the man in action.

Foxx put the food on the table and blessed the table. He was way different than the man I thought he was. I wanted to say a lot but I just didn't know how to say what I wanted to say. I was glad when Foxx continued the discussion.

"Damian, I don't tell anyone this, including my kids, but Stone and I have been friends since we were kids. Maybe a little older than when you and Reggie became friends. But Stone taught me about life, and about living. He even made me his counsel, if you will. We were thick as thieves."

I smiled. Listening to Foxx talk about Stone made me think about the bond Reggie and I built over the years. That nigga saved me from over a dozen bullets. I just wished that I was around to protect him before Miguel snatched him up. Fighting for his life was the least I could do.

INTERNATIONALLY KNOWN

"Damian I shared all of this for one reason and that is, let me be your consultant, your old age counselor. If you follow my lead, everything will work out for everybody." He said and then he fell silent.

I accepted that, I was cool with that, but I knew there was something else on Foxx's mind that he wasn't saying or hadn't said yet. So I pressed the issue. "What else is it Foxx? I can tell you have something else we need to discuss . . . I want you to know that we can talk about anything."

"Thanks son, appreciate that," Foxx replied.

"So what's up?" I asked.

"What we are doing goes in stages, Damian. I want you to realize that." He looked at me eye-to-eye and I didn't know where this was going, but I was ready for anything. "When we do meet with Miguel Chavez, Naomi needs to be with us. Miguel needs to know we mean business and the person he deems to be the weakest, is Naomi. But after all hell breaks loose, he will finally see what she is made of. He needs to know whether it's Reggie or Naomi, we stand tall and we stand strong."

I understood. I knew where he was coming from. I hadn't thought about it, but I would have gotten there on my own. If Reggie survived this as well as Naomi and I, we were going to be a strong team if Reggie also bought off on the new dynamic.

No more words were spoken. Foxx excused himself and told me he was going to the basement to check on the kids. Before he exited the kitchen, he grabbed two plates of food and left. I went and sat in the living room and chilled.

I didn't realized I had dozed off on the sofa until I felt Naomi's soft kisses all over my face and neck. I blinked my eyes to clear my vision and then I zoomed in on her. She smiled at me from ear to ear. Plus she smelled good. I instantly saw that she had showered and changed into a new set of clothes. "You smell so good." I complimented her.

"I wish I could say the same for you," she smiled at me. I knew she was pulling my leg. But she did have a point.

"Why don't you run me some bath water?" I asked her.

"Let's go," she told me.

After she escorted me to the bathroom near the bedroom we shared, I got undressed and got into the shower. It felt good. I told Naomi I needed to feel the hot water cascading down my body and she made it happen. I needed to get my senses rejuvenated. And that's what I did.

The shower definitely did a body good. In fact, it loosened my mind. I was on the here and now, and begun to think about how we would proceed. As the hot water attacked my body and I washed my dick and balls, it came to me. I knew what we were going to do. After all, I was the leader for now.

I told both Foxx and Naomi my plan and it blew them away. It was genius. But Foxx hit me below the belt when he broke the news to Naomi and I that he had a few people put out the word on the streets that

Pretty Pedro kidnapped Dante's son, and in return, Dante did the same to Pretty Pedro by kidnapping his daughter. I was blown away and thought that that plan was more genius than mine. Additionally, Dante' had killed his four bodyguards who were supposedly protecting his baby mama and his son.

The most important news of all was the two drug dealers were at odds with each other. The simple fact our names were not mentioned or thought of was a positive for us. The next move was on us and we made it.

Our plans changed from me making the calls to Dante' and Pretty Pedro to Foxx doing it. In my mind, Foxx was a better fit. Foxx was a master at disguising his voice. Foxx could impersonate anyone. So our plan was for him to impersonate the actor Al Pacino who starred in the role of Scarface when he called the men and made the ransom. Plus, we were going to put the kids on the phone to add pressure to their fathers. We planned to give the kids fifteen seconds to cry their poor hearts out and then we'd end the call. Sticking and moving was all we needed to do. And now it was time to see if the plan would work.

"Who the fuck is this?" Dante asked rudely through the speakerphone as if he was a man who was pissed and on edge. Even though his voice sounded intimidating, we could still the pain in his voice. He made it no secret that he wanted to kill someone.

"This is the man who will be delivering your son," Foxx said in his best Scarface voice. "And to get him back I want a half-million dollars in two days."

"Who is this goddammit?" the man nicknamed D.D. asked again.

"I'm the man who will be five hundred thousand dollars richer in two days," Foxx replied. "I will call you in two days with the details."

Before Foxx could hang up, D.D. screamed, "I can get the money in less than twenty-four hours! Let's do this! I want my son back nigga!"

Foxx gave me the thumbs up. "I will call back tomorrow or the next day and give you details. If my instructions are not followed to the letter, I will deliver your son to you in a body bag."

We all had our game faces on when Foxx got off the phone. Foxx had already told us he had the perfect drop site. Now it was time to get Pretty Pedro on the phone.

"Is this the motherfucker that has my baby girl, Toshiba?" Pretty Pedro asked smoothly.

"Yes it is," Foxx aka Scarface voice said. "And it will take a half-million dollars to get her back. I will call you in two days and give you the details."

"Listen, D.D., or whoever this is, I didn't take your son," Pretty Pedro rebutted. "I want my daughter back and I don't mind paying. A half-mil ain't shit to me! So, I want you to know that I don't kidnap kids. Shit we all agreed that families are off-limits. But I want my kid back and I'm not looking for a war. Just know that if you want war, you know I'm damn good at it."

"I will call you back tomorrow or the next day," Foxx replied.

"Can I speak to my daughter," Pedro responded. "Proof of life."

Foxx put his daughter on the phone and let them talk for fifteen to twenty seconds. "Daddy. Daddy. Please come get me," she cried.

"Are you all right baby? Have they touched you?" Pedro yelled.

"Daddy, I'm scared. I want you to and come get me now." she continued to cry.

Pedro realized that it didn't matter how much he told her it was going to be all right, there was no way he'd be able to console her. And when Foxx took the phone back from her, she screamed to the top of her voice and Pedro went off the deep end. "You better not touch my motherfucking daughter! You hear me? I swear if anything happens to her, I'm gonna kill you nigga. And I'm gonna kill you slow!" he screamed.

"She has been fed, bathed and taken care of. We are not trying to hurt her. This is strictly business . . . you will hear from me."

After Foxx hung up the phone, he took the kids to the basement. I wondered why Dante didn't ask about his son. I lost even more respect for his bitch ass.

When Foxx returned, we all knew one thing— our plan had to be foolproof. If not, Pretty Pedro would probably kill us all. Overall, the man didn't assign niggas to his family because no one fucked with him and his loved ones.

I could only ask myself, were we in over our heads?

KIKI SWINSON

Naomi's Running Shit

I had volunteered to oversee the little people, Lil Toshiba and D'Marcus. It was a joy just to see the two intermingle considering their circumstances. Toshiba was only three but she related well to D'Marcus, who was six. He was a tough little kid but he was only a kid who wanted to be older than he was. He reminded me so much of Reggie. He was protecting Toshiba, and that's what Reggie used to do for me.

In a perfect world, Toshiba and D'Marcus would never find out that their fathers were enemies. Hopefully in that same world, maybe the two of them would meet each other in twenty to twenty-five years and become friends or maybe, lovers. I smiled at the thought. Hell, I was still a woman and I still had romantic and lovable thoughts.

In a perfect world, all things were possible . . . even retrieving my brother from a greedy ass, South American gangster.

I was donning a Condoleezza Rice mask with a wig that was so similar to her hairdo. Needless to say I looked older. The kids didn't seem to mind, probably because I was a woman and more gentle than Damian and younger than my father. Our goal was to make sure the kids didn't see our real faces or any distinguishing marks. Even with kids, we didn't want them to know anything that could come back and get us killed.

My dad had hit the streets and been on the horn finding out as much information as possible. We knew the police had tried to get involved; including the FBI, but Pretty Pedro and D.D. had both refused to say their kids had been kidnapped. In the world we lived in, it was a huge sign of weakness if the *proverbial man* had to handle your business for you. But just knowing that information meant we had to be extra careful now. Although the cops weren't invited to the party meant they would stake out Pedro's and D.D.'s places for information, and more relevant to us, movement of people.

Our world was crumpling around us. The sharks were circling and we didn't budge or let it deter us from handling our business. Hell, we knew reputations were on the line as well. So we had to have a foolproof plan to make shit happen the way we wanted it to happen.

This was day three of our deadline to get the money that would get Reggie released. We had a plan and had discussed it repeatedly. We had it down to the last minute. If this was our last stand, it had to be a good one.

Meanwhile, the word was buzzing that six drug dealers' operations were hit yesterday, including the shit that went down at D.D.'s place and Pretty Pedro's. The ironic thing was that D.D.'s shit was the worse, but Pretty Pedro's was the real buzz. No one fucked with Pretty Pedro. All truces had been broken with the shit we did. Although the only thing we did was take his daughter and steal fifty thousand from his home, without hurting anyone, Pretty Pedro was Mr. Untouchable in our business. He rose up when Reggie's operation had gone tits up. Where Reggie used to be the untouchable one, now it was Pretty Pedro. He was the organizer of the truce between the criminal elements. He brokered the deal and smooth talked the other dealers to coming to the table and divvying up the territory.

Now we had fucked that all up. If all went well, they would never know it was us, but with shit like this, all never goes well. We had to pay the piper one day . . . I just hoped one day was not sooner than later.

It was around nine that night and we had decided not to hit any other operation tonight. Our goal was to call the kids' fathers tomorrow morning and make the drop then. We had everything worked out to ninety minutes, a good hour and a half. The faster we got the kids off our hands, the faster we could get back to our Bonnie and Clyde act, if that was possible.

The three dealers we hadn't hit yet were tops on the list of possible suspects. D.D. and Pretty Pedro weren't sure if the other had done the kidnapping and the other one retaliated. But once the kids were returned, they would know neither one of them were responsible for this madness. With four of the other operations being hit, it would be down to the three that weren't hit.

INTERNATIONALLY KNOWN

Additionally, there was a buzz out there that maybe Miguel was trying to make a point. Everyone by now knew he had Reggie and the thought was he kidnapped the two top dogs' kids to send a message. My father hadn't heard if that rumor had grown legs and taken off. I didn't think it had. I really didn't think anyone wanted to mess with Marco. Although only a select few of people knew him personally in the New York area, everyone knew his reputation. He was not the person to be fucked with.

And if all of this didn't go over right, as in Reggie was hurt or killed, we would be messing with Marco, because his son would be a dead man. That was my promise, even if it took me to the grave, Miguel would be joining me six feet under.

"I never knew life could be so well," I said to Damian in my dream. We were chilling in a park, watching our two kids, a boy and a girl, roughly around the same age. Our kids looked like us when we were younger. Damian was sitting with his back to a tree and I was lying down cuddled in his strong arms. Our kids were running around and we were just enjoying life.

I didn't know what it meant. And honestly, I didn't care. I wanted to enjoy the moment, whether it was a dream or not. Who knew what the future had in store for us? I didn't know whether I was hormonal, PMS'ing or what. I didn't know why I was questioning my dream. I didn't even know if my parents even wanted grandchildren. I didn't know if I really wanted kids. So what was this dream all about?

I remember growing up happy as a kid. We had the best of all worlds. I grew up around love. My parents absolutely loved each other. That was a good thing—is a good thing. I wanted what they had. I was hoping Damian was indeed the one for me. I still wasn't sure I wanted the whole family unit but I was willing to play it a day at a time.

When I woke up around four that morning, my dream was still fresh on my mind. It put a smile on my face. That shit would rock if one day Damian and I had our own family. Maybe it was just a thought. We had to make it through this day. Something told me all hell was going to break out after this morning.

Thank God, we were on the road by five in three separate cars. The plan was in motion and I wanted to get this thing over and done with. We knew what we were dealing with. My father had another brilliant idea. The most amazing thing was I had a lot of confidence that his brilliant idea would work, which meant it was indeed – foolproof.

The night before when we had called D.D. and Pretty Pedro and had them talk to their kids on speakerphones, we used a new throwaway phone every time we called one of the drug dealers. This time around when we called D.D. we had to force him to talk to D'Marcus. When he did, I could hear the crack in the man's voice. He loved his son and it hurt him that he couldn't do anything to help his son. Immediately after their call ended, we got Pedro back on the line.

INTERNATIONALLY KNOWN

After their exchanges with the kids, my father talked to each man in his disguised Scarface voice and told each man to expect more instructions tomorrow. Then he told each of them to go outside to their cars and inside their cars, on the back seat, was a medium size duffel bag with a shoulder strap. D.D.'s duffel bag was black and Pedro's bag was black with a white stripe on each side of the bag. The bags were for the money. He gave them specific instructions to stack the money neatly in the bags and to expect a call any time between five the next morning to three the next afternoon. It was an intentional ten-hour window to fuck with each man.

By six that morning, we were all in place and ready to rock. This was it. The time was now. We were back on our conference connections with our Bluetooth and earpieces. When he made the phone call, we all listened in.

"Yeah," Pedro said. His voice was alert. We could tell that he was waiting on the call. He was with his boys at a duplex in the Bronx so we knew what time it was. He and his boys were ready to snatch us up as soon as we made our first move. Therefore, our move had to be the right move.

"Pedro, have your wife, go outside and walk down the street and she will see a burgundy 2000 Nissan Maxima," my father explained still using his Scarface voice.

"Hold on, what the fuck you mean, have my wife walk down the street? I'm not involving her in this shit!" Pedro's voice raised an octave. But he continued on, disregarding anything Pedro was trying to say.

"The key is under the floor mat on the driver's seat and inside the glove compartment is a throwaway cell phone. On the passenger's seat are her directions. If anyone else gets in the car besides your wife, or if someone jumps in the car with her, your daughter is dead. And if she tries to text you or call you, your daughter is dead."

"Nigga, you threatening me?" Pedro boomed.

Once again Foxx disregarded Pedro and continued to make his demands. And this made Pedro even angrier. "Do you hear what the fuck I am telling you?" He roared.

"Pedro, your best bet is to hear what I am saying. The quicker we can get through this, the quicker you can see your daughter again." he informed him.

"But I told you I wasn't involving my wife and you just talked all over me."

"I'm sorry but I can not make any exceptions. The plan was for your wife to handle the transaction and that's how it will be." My father explained. "Now are you ready for me to continue?" he continued.

"Man hurry the fuck up and let's get this shit over with." Pedro replied sarcastically.

"I'm gonna need your right hand man, Bowser, to get in his Beemer and meet your wife and give her the money. And if Bowser tries to follow her, your daughter will die. And so you know, they only have fifteen minutes to hook up, starting now."

Pedro tried saying something, but my father had hung up the phone. He stayed on the outskirts of the Bronx. He was a good twenty to thirty minutes away from his home. He had two bodyguards staying at his place, watching over his wife. But we had fucked up his plans. It was going to be on her to deliver the money. When his henchmen jumped in their car to try to follow his wife, they would find out fast that the car had two flat tires and the oil pan had a hole in it, thus no oil in the car.

After the call ended with Pedro, my father called Dante's phone next. "Who dis?" a tired and sleepy D.D. answered the phone.

"Have your right hand man, Mason, go to BSR #1 parking lot and find a burnt orange 1995 Mustang."

"What the fuck is up," D.D. tried intervening. He and his men were huddled up at BSR #4, including his main man, Mason. They were waiting on our call to the first building parking lot would take a good five minutes or so to get to the car. That's why we used burnt orange, something easier to find.

"Why the fuck you said that nigga's name?" D.D. continued. "Are you working with Mason on this shit?"

"Listen, asshole," my father replied. I was loving the Scarface voice. It was hard for me not to laugh. "I call the fucking shots and you listen or your son is dead. Now shut the fuck up!"

"The key is under the floor mat on the driver's seat and inside the glove compartment is a throwaway cell phone. On the passenger's seat are his directions.

If any of your men try to follow, your son is dead. If Mason tries to text or call you, your son is dead. He has ten minutes, starting now."

Then he hung up the phone.

The instructions informed Pedro's wife and Dante's right hand man to throw their personal cell phones out the window and pick up the phone on the passenger's seat. When they looked at the phone, the first thing that would come up would be directions to their first location. The instructions also told them the only way they could use the phone was lose the directions. Pedro's wife wasn't going to fuck up like that, she loved her daughter and no way was she going to jeopardize anything dealing with her safe return. I figured Mason wouldn't fuck up either. He was D'Marcus godfather so now he was responsible for carrying that weight on his shoulders.

At their first location, they would both transfer cars to other cars. My dad had set it up that as soon as the cars were dropped off, someone would pick up the cars and get them back to New Jersey. My father had told his guys to only pick up the cars if no cops were around as well as members of D.D.'s or Pretty Pedro's gangs.

My father followed the same routine as before: the key was under the floor mat, another phone in the glove compartment and new instructions on the passenger's seat. The next instruction was to throw away the last phone, then follow the directions on the new phone. The directions would take them to the nearest subway, and they had a certain amount of time to get to the subway station.

From there, it was simple. Get off on Wall Street. This was the best part. They would take their respective bags to South Street on the East End of Wall Street. This was golden. Foot traffic during this time of morning from the three subway systems in Manhattan's money district was atrocious. There were literally thousands of people trying to get from Point A to Point B.

My dad's final instructions included putting the duffel bags in a trashcan on Second Street. The irony was Pedro's wife and Mason would put their bags in the trashcan within seconds of each other. The two looked at each other. They knew each other. They were former lovers . . . lovers who actually loved each other. But they were from different parts of New York, different Boroughs.

My dad told me he had seen this trashcan scenario in a movie. The trashcan was placed over a manhole cover. We had removed the cover, when they dropped the bags in the trashcan, both me and Damian was below in an empty corridor of the subway work areas.

We had gloves on, along with a mask that even covered our eyes. This was just in case there was some kind of exploding paint or something in the duffel bags. Additionally, we were transferring the money into another bag in case there was some kind of honing device in the bag or between the money. And indeed, in both bags, there were cell phones that we were sure had GPS technology. He took the bags and ran towards the subway.

We took our bag of one million dollars and went about our way. We told my dad all was good as we hauled ass through the subway tunnel, following directions given to us by him. He in turn called both Pedro's wife and Mason and told them to walk down to Pier 11 and the kids would be sleep in a silver and black rental car.

In a perfect world, all things are possible.

INTERNATIONALLY KNOWN

INTERNATIONALLY KNOWN:
NEW YORK'S FINEST (PART 2)

KIKI SWINSON

Damian's Time To Chill

I was shocked! We actually did it! We pulled this shit off.

Running through the tunnel and eventually making our way to the street, I still wasn't sure we would get away with it. But we did. We succeeded in getting the job done. I was proud of our success. Hell, I was proud of our teamwork and everything we had done since we had made our way back to New York.

We were still short eight hundred thousand dollars. We had a plan. But it would wait for a day. Things were crazy in the city. As soon as Pretty Pedro and Dante got their kids back, all hell broke out. They realized that they didn't kidnap each other's kids, so they supposedly had a sit down to figure this shit out.

The good thing was the kids couldn't tell them anything. I don't know what was what, but evidently the breakfast Foxx had made that morning put the kids to sleep and screwed with their short term memory. That fucking Foxx was something else. I didn't know if he learned everything from Stone or if he knew shit on his own. Whatever it was, I could see the two of them as a team.

KIKI SWINSON

I was feeling good as hell. We got back to the house around eleven. Foxx wasn't in the house long before he hit the streets. I think both Naomi and I were happy he left. We gave him five minutes. Then it was on.

Naomi and I were on each other like white on rice. We were still downstairs and kissing hard. It wasn't a one thing leads to another . . . we knew what the *another* was. We were about to do some serious fucking. We were kissing as we worked our way up the stairs. We both fell when we got to the top step and laughed it off. It really was funny.

We made it to the bedroom and started taking each other's clothes off. We were sweaty. Neither one of us had hit the shower yet, and guess what, we didn't give a damn. When Naomi dropped to her knees and put my dick in her mouth, I felt alive. I loved the way this woman sucked my dick. She usually gave me the whole experience. From putting my whole dick in her mouth, which absolutely drove my ass crazy, to doing magical shit with her tongue on the tip of my dick to even sucking my balls, Naomi was an expert at curling my damn toes.

I don't know how long she sucked my dick. I just know there were several times I tried to push her away. She knew I couldn't handle that shit all day. That was one of our things, to see which one of us could make who come first. I was good at holding my own, whereas Naomi loved my mouth and tongue and I had her screaming like a banshee within five to ten minutes of eating her pussy.

INTERNATIONALLY KNOWN

But this time was different. Naomi was deep throating me and that was kicking my ass. And she was doing that shit faster and faster. I didn't know what to do with my hands. I had my right hand on the back of her head. It was just there. She didn't need my assistance. Her speed and her movements were within her control and I loved her control.

I knew I was in trouble when I put both of my hands on the back of her head. Then it happened. "Fuck, fuck, fuck!" I said aloud. "Shit . . . fuck! Suck that dick baby, suck that dick! Dammmmnnnnn!"

I honestly had no idea how in the hell I was still standing. My legs were weak and wobbly. Naomi was a swallower and I loved that about her. She was still munching at my dick and I was trying to get her to stop. When I was finally able to get her to her feet, we went over to the bed.

I laid down flat on my back and pulled Naomi to sit on my face. I loved that shit. I loved when she sat that nice ass and juicy lips on my face. And I loved it more when she started grinding that ass on my face. I attacked her clit with my tongue first, licking it and then chewing on that shit. Then I tongue fucked that pussy. Just like she had her tricks when she sucked my dick, I had the same thing: my tricks.

I gripped her ass with both of my hands and continued to eat that sloppy, wet pussy. I could feel my dick getting new life. It wasn't hard yet but it had new feeling. By the time I was through eating that pussy, I knew my shit would be full of lead. So I kept eating Naomi's pussy like a death row inmate eating a last meal. When I stuck two fingers in her and sucked on that clit that was it. She was in another universe.

"Oh, shit," she moaned. "Gimme . . . gimme . . . that . . . dick." When she finally got those words out, I knew she would be coming soon as she bucked that ass. "Fuck D . . . fuck. I'm . . . I'm . . . shit." She couldn't get the words out, but her body tightened up, and then relaxed. I was still munching that pussy and she was trying her best to still move that ass. I guess our morning of being bad guys had sapped our energy. Usually, we would still be ready for a serious round of fucking after orally pleasing each other. But it was all good. My dick at last had new energy. I was wondering about Naomi, when she said, "I still want that dick."

I slide my face from underneath her ass and took that shit doggy style. Just seeing that pussy all sloppy and wet and knowing my contribution to the cause made my dick harder. Naomi pushed that ass back towards to me and I could tell she was tired as shit, but like me, horny as hell. I did what I was supposed to do and that was sticking my dick as deep as I could go into that pussy.

I think a couple of things women loved about me was that I could hold my own in the bedroom and I was a man of a hundred and one positions. And that afternoon, we went through a number of positions from regular doggie to me holding Naomi's ankles to one side and me standing while she laid on the bed. Not only did my dick have new life, I was reenergized. I didn't know what had come over me. Maybe it was the simple fact of all the shit we had done together, as a couple, and then celebrating with some old fashioned serious fucking.

I don't know how long we went at it. I know I was tired as shit when we finally collapsed. Our bedroom door was closed and locked for security reasons. The last thing I ever wanted to do was disrespect Foxx. Having him see me laid up with his daughter butt ass naked would definitely do the trick.

Sleep was good. I didn't know what Naomi was dreaming about, but evidently it was good because she snuggled up to me. I didn't remember going to sleep with her in my arms, but she was now. And I was very cool with that. I had never thought about making any bitch my wife in the past, but with Naomi it was different. I didn't know if she ever had thoughts about that. We never talked about it. Plus, we didn't know our situation right now. Shit, we could be dead tomorrow. Hell, we could be dead tonight if Dante' and Pedro knew where to find us.

We were awakened out of our sleep by a banging on the bedroom door. "You two, get the hell up, we need to talk!" Foxx blasted.

Naomi and I jumped out of bed and scrambled to put on our clothes. Immediately after, we threw water on our faces and rinsed our mouths with mouthwash. Something told me this wasn't good from the tone in Foxx's voice. When we got downstairs, he was in the kitchen, waiting on the coffee to finish brewing.

"We need to lay low," were the first words out of his mouth when we entered into the room. His tone was flat, his demeanor edgy. Something wasn't right. "Pedro and that young cat Dante; have been busy since they got their kids back. Besides starting a war up in Harlem, Bedford-Stuy and East New York, Miguel Chavez ordered a sit down with Dante' and Pedro after he heard about the heist. And that dirty fuck told Pedro and D.D. that he had Reggie and demanded five million from us and that he knew we had to be behind the kidnapping and the robberies. So, there's word on the streets that Dante' and Pedro have both put one hundred thousand dollar bounties on our head for anyone who turns us in."

"Fuck," was the only thing Naomi could say.

"Shit, Foxx, we are eight hundred thousand short," I said. "This kinda fucks up our plan. What are we gonna do?"

"We need to lay low."

"I don't understand this shit," Naomi chimed in. "This motherfucker wants five mil from us but he's turning us in and making this shit harder. What the fuck is he thinking?"

And that's when it hit me. "Foxx, your wife, we need to go get her," I said excitedly as I had jumped up and was ready to move.

"Calm down, Damian, she is already en route to Chicago with her niece," Foxx replied. "I took care of that shit as soon as I heard what was up. I wasn't going to give them a chance to fuck with my wife after we invaded their households; I knew they would do

INTERNATIONALLY KNOWN

the same to us. For now, we just need to lay low for a couple of days. This shit has just gotten more complicated, but we will prevail."

"What do you think is going on?" Naomi asked her father.

"I think Miguel want us all dead," he replied quickly. "I think he wants to prove a point. That he is the big dog in New York. He put shit in motion and we fell into the trap. I think he knew the only way we could get money like this if we didn't have it stashed away was rob other dealers. Then I think he was gonna put the word out that we did this shit, not expecting us to even come close to getting the money we needed for Reggie. Then when we snatched the kids, we made it better for Miguel. That started a war that he squashed and put the ball in our court. Except the ball is flat and we can't bounce it."

"Then we have only one thing left to do," I began. "That is kill Miguel and let motherfuckers know that we mean business."

"No, Damian, that's not the way to go," Naomi stated. "Dad is right, we need to lay low for a day or two. We have been doing some reckless shit but no more. We need to plan this shit right. For us and for Reggie. And since mom is on her way to Chicago we won't have to worry about her safety." She looked at Foxx and he cracked a half smile.

"You are absolutely right. So for now, let's just chill." He agreed.

I looked at Naomi and I was surprised to see her give orders. She was the calm one. She was the one thinking smartly. I thought she would be all up in tears and emotional. This was what Stone, Reggie and Foxx wanted to see from her when they mentioned this shit in the hospital. Miguel and Marco had shitted on her during one of Marco's visits to New York, and they were convinced she couldn't lead the operation if anything ever happened to Reggie.

Well, they were wrong.

My baby was in control.

INTERNATIONALLY KNOWN

INTERNATIONALLY KNOWN: NEW YORK'S FINEST (PART 2)

KIKI SWINSON

Naomi's Time to Shine

I had the first security shift, from ten to one. We had agreed to get some sleep and set up three-hour security shifts. I had music playing in the background. The volume was turned down low. I was playing Blackjack on my laptop computer. It was just a distraction. I was alert and ready for anything. I had a Glock 27 and Glock 40 on one side of me, and an AR-15 assault rifle on the other side. Not to mention, I had my two Taser guns at my disposal.

I had several things on my mind. Actually, I had a lot of things on my mind. My mind was literally all over the place. But for whatever reason, my mind kept going back to one thought. Looking down at my small arsenal, memories of my dad and Stone taking me out shooting on numerous occasions flooded my mind. I think the first time I held a gun in my hand I was probably six or seven years old. I was dismissed from school for fighting that day. My father had picked me up and Stone was waiting for us in the car.

I will never forget when my father had asked me what happened and I told him a boy had pulled my ponytail and I beat him up. My dad had heard the teacher's version of what happened, but that was the relationship my father and I had at an early age. My word was the word he respected. Even if it was bad he wanted me to tell him the truth, and that's what I done. He asked me did the boy like me or if I liked the boy. I told him no because I wasn't into boys then.

Stone and my father took me to a field out in the boonies of New Jersey. At that time, Stone had a big, dark blue, four-door Mercedes Benz. When they parked and got out of the car, I didn't have a clue what was going on. When they went to the back of the car and opened the trunk, my eyes grew big. Stone had two big duffel type bags of guns, all kinds of guns. Of course at six or seven I couldn't tell you the difference between a handgun and a rifle.

My dad gave me two big plastic bags of cans and told me to go put them on a fence about thirty or forty yards away. It was a three rail fence and he told me to put cans on all three rails. I took one bag and it was heavy. Stone asked me what was I doing and I told him I was doing what my daddy told me to do. He told me no, to take both bags at the same time, and I should have thought about that before I beat up the boy. This was punishment. I know both were proud I could take care of myself, but both men wanted me to know there are always consequences to my acts of defiance.

I don't know when my father stopped liking guns, but I remember him being able to shoot perfectly. He and Stone played their shooting game and both men didn't miss a shot. Of course being so young I was easily impressed but I knew then I wanted to be able to shoot like that one day. And I never thought that day would be my first lesson.

My father told me the small gun was a .25 caliber handgun. My hands were small but I could grip the gun halfway decently with both hands. My dad taught me about lining up the sights and keeping the gun steady. He took me through some trigger exercises, schooling me on the kickback of the gun. Even in the open field, we had earplugs in our ears and I could tell how loud guns could be. He explained to me that most people couldn't shoot straight because they anticipated the explosion of the weapon. And I understood. I too was jerking the gun just doing trigger exercises. When my dad thought I was ready, he told me he would give me six shots.

We moved up to about ten yards away from the fence. Stone set up six cans on the second rail. I didn't know if he really had confidence in me then or just wanted me to have confidence. Pulling the trigger the first time with a bullet in the chamber completely shocked the hell out of me. Crazily, I hit a can but not the one I was aiming for. It was two cans to the right. Foxx gave me more instructions on controlling my breathing and teaching me breathing, hand and finger control should all be in sync with each other. And even at a young age I understood what he was saying.

My next four shots I didn't hit anything. But I was surprised when my dad nor Stone gave up on me. Stone was telling me on the sideline to stay with it, don't give up. He continued to give me directions. My hands were hurting a little bit but no way was I giving up. I listened to everything Foxx was telling me and I was trying my best to do so.

Then he whispered something in my ear, "Come on, lil' lady, if your brother can do this, I know you can."

For whatever reason, that did encourage me. I did everything he had told me to do and I was surprised and happy when I hit the can I was trying to shoot. My dad leaned down, and kissed me on the top of my head and took the gun from me. Stone came and swept me off my feet, and gave me a kiss on the forehead. Then he carried me to the fence and he and I collected the cans and put them in the two big trash bags. This time Stone carried the two bags to the car.

I didn't know why that particular dream came back to me, but I remembered everything my dad and Stone used to talk about back in those days. Mostly during our shooting range trips, it was all about shooting. But occasionally, both men would make sure they threw in something about life and life's lessons. And I realized those lessons were for me. Those lessons would shape my life. Those lessons kept me alive. Those lessons had to continue to keep me alive.

Damian relieved me at one and I think my dad did that on purpose. He didn't want us fucking when I went to bed and then when Damian relieved him at four he would be tired. So Damian relieved me at one. I told him everything was cool and pretty quiet. He asked me what I did to keep awake and I told him I played Blackjack.

My man wasn't into the computer, only when it came to business. Doing recreational things on the computer wasn't something that thrilled Damian. I was cool with that. I kinda laughed at the whole thing. Reggie was a big time computer geek, so were a couple of the other dope dealers we knew. Computers for many drug dealers were used for accounting purposes. I was sure the other dealers were doing the same thing Reggie used to do, keep his laptop at his hideaway crib . . . the one location no one really knew about.

But I didn't stick around and bullshit with Damian. I took my ass to bed. I was tired and I still had plenty of thoughts on my mind. I laughed at the craziness of my attitude from the time we made it back to this area. First, I was scared shitless and didn't want to be here. Now, I was in control and full of life. I kept thinking about my dream of being the warrior bitch and rescuing Reggie from a warehouse with Damian and Stone by my side. Now I realized that it wasn't Stone by my side, but my dad. Even though my dad wasn't a gunman, he loved his kids. Reggie was his only son. I knew my father would be by our side when the time came to get Reggie back.

In my dream, I was walking through the Butler Sky Rise shooting motherfuckers. Like any dream, much of it didn't make sense. I only had two guns with me, but whenever I ran out of bullets, I didn't reload; I just pulled two new guns out of my pants' pockets. I didn't even have a clue why I was shooting motherfuckers in the BSRs. But I was going from building to building just killing bitch ass niggas. Then I saw who

I was looking for. It was D'Marcus. He was playing with a little girl, who I immediately realized was Lil Toshiba. They ran to me and hugged me when they saw me. I was completely dumbfounded and clueless. I didn't know why I was rescuing them or why they even needed rescuing, but they were happy to see me and even wanted to go with me.

So we made our way back through the BSRs. For whatever reason, we were working our way from up to down in every building. It truly was a dream. In the real world, I would have taken a direct route. But in my dream, I was taking the longest route possible. I was still killing folks as if I was in a video game just killing folks. A couple of times instead of reaching into my pockets for new weapons, I reached in and just recharged my weapons, and came right back firing.

We had made it through each building and had finally reached the parking lot. I got the kids in my old SUV. I had no idea where the whip came from, but I was happy I had it back. After I got in the car and I thought all was good, standing in front of me was Miguel Chavez and in his hand was a Glock 40 aimed at me. Before I could react and grab my weapon, Miguel fired his weapon and I could see the bullet headed directly for my heart.

I woke up suddenly from that apparent nightmare. I noticed Damian was still knocked out. I looked at the clock and it read nine fifteen. I didn't want to wake up Damian, so I tried to be as quiet as possible. I did my thing in the bathroom, including brushing my teeth. I didn't want to take a shower yet and wake up my man.

As I made my way downstairs, I heard my dad talking to someone in the kitchen. I smelled food as well but something wasn't right. I didn't think he was on the phone, so I was very concerned. I saw my guns still on the sofa, so I quietly walked to the sofa and picked up the Glock 27. I was in a nightshirt with gym shorts on and slippers. Trust me, that wasn't going to stop me from shooting a gun.

I continued to move lightly, quietly towards the kitchen. I couldn't make out the conversation. Momentarily, I thought maybe I was making a mistake not waking up Damian. Shit, it was too late now. I had to continue on my quest. If my father was in trouble and something happened to him, I would feel like shit.

I moved as if I was a fucking detective woman on a mission to apprehend or kill the perpetrator. I took a breath before I entered the kitchen with my weapon in the ready to fire position. Then my mouth flew open with shock. What the fuck!

"Uncle Stone!" I yelled with excitement as I ran into the tall man's arms and gave him the biggest bear hug. We hugged for a while. My dad took that opportunity to take the Glock out of my hand. "What in the hell is going on? I thought you were dead," I said as I looked back at my dad, who was sitting at the table eating breakfast.

"No, it takes a lot to kill an old head like me, baby girl," Stone said. He smiled as he continued to hug and hold me with one arm. "Sit down and let me get you some breakfast."

I did as I was told. "Damn, how in the hell did you escape?" I asked.

"Well, no way I was blowing up myself to save your sorry asses," he smiled, giving me the biggest smile he could muster up. It was nice to see. I think I was one of the very few people to see Stone smile more than once. "I set the explosives and was making my way out of the building, when I heard a television blasting in one of the apartments. The FBI had done a good job of evacuating everyone out of the building except this particular building. So I kicked down the door and found two kids watching TV and their mom was sleep in the bedroom. I grabbed the kids and their mom and we made our way out of the building the same way you guys did. Unfortunately, I suffered some minor burns on my back and the back of my legs. So the woman I rescued was able to help me get to my car."

"Well, where the hell have you been all this time?"

"For the past several months, I have been chilling down in the Caribbean. Foxx gave me a call when Reggie was taken and told me to get back as soon as I could. We have been talking ever since this shit kicked off."

I was blown away. This shit was crazy. I thought maybe I was dreaming, so I pinched myself. Yep, I was wide awake. "This is fucking crazy, this shit can't be real."

"Trust me, it's real and I'm very much alive," Stone said.

I looked at my father and said, "Dad why didn't you tell us Stone was till alive?"

"It wasn't the right time baby."

"Well, when were you going to tell me?" I pressed the issue.

"Now," he said and turned his attention towards Stone.

"Listen Naomi, a lot of stuff has happened since that day everyone separated. And it was very important for your father and I to keep my whereabouts a secret until the time was right. And now was that time."

"Are you gonna help us get Reggie back?"

"What kind of question is that? Of course, I am going to get Reggie back. And from listening to your father, it sounds like you guys have gotten yourselves into some crazy shit."

I sighed heavily. "Yep, that's what it seems like."

"Well baby girl, don't worry because your father and I are about to take this madness to a different level. Question is, are you ready?"

I smiled. "Yes I am," I said with confidence.

Stone and my father looked at each other and gave each other a smile. Stone seemed different to me. I don't know what it was. In just the little time we had spent in the kitchen, it seemed . . . happy. Not that Stone didn't already have it all, but the man never seemed like he was happy. In just a few months, something had happened to change all of that.

"You know, I have been thinking a lot about you, Uncle Stone, and I remember the first time you and my dad took me shooting as well as the other times we went shooting. I think those outings defined my life. You guys taught me so much about life and I think I actually lived my life based on the stuff you two taught me."

"If that's a thank you, baby girl, you're welcome," Stone said.

"I do have one question though."

"What's that," Stone replied.

"No, it's for my dad," I said.

"Oh, really." My dad interjected. "What's your question?" he asked.

"Why do you dislike guns so much? I remember when we used to go shooting when I was young. You were a great shooter. You could shoot just as good as Uncle Stone. Plus, you loved shooting. Then one day, you just stopped wanting to shoot. I don't get it, what happened."

My father looked at me. It was almost as if he was looking right through me. I noticed Stone drinking coffee and looking at my dad but my dad put his head down for a minute. I didn't know if he was thinking or what. I realized that something happened to caused him to stop shooting.

"Yeah, I always loved guns, Pumpkin," he began. "This crazy S-O-B taught me how to shoot when we were probably fourteen, fifteen or sixteen years old. Hell, it's been so long I can't even remember when."

I noticed my father's face had tensed up. He was serious. Something told me he didn't want to talk about it, but he would do it—for me. Plus, I couldn't remember the last time he called me Pumpkin. That was my nickname when I was growing up for years. Now, he only called me that occasionally, whereas my mom called me that all the time.

"You remember when you were probably twelve or thirteen and your mom went to Chicago for a couple of months?"

"Yeah."

"Well, your mom was assaulted," my dad said solemnly.

"What?" I was totally caught by surprise.

"I was paid some pretty good money to break in this rich guy's house in the suburbs of Trenton. I stole some high price jewelry. It was a pretty good payday for me. But the guy I stole the jewelry for, lied to his partners and said I kept several pieces for myself. Well, one day three of his guys came to our old apartment and roughed up your mom."

"They didn't rape her, did they?" I asked. I don't know why, but that was important to me.

"No, they didn't," he responded immediately. "Probably only because our next door neighbor, Gilbert, heard them kick the door open and grabbed his gun and came over to your mom's rescue. Unfortunately, they shot Gilbert but your mom was able to make it to the bedroom and lock the door. Because of the shooting, the men got the hell out of the apartment, afraid someone was going to call the police."

"Man, I remember Mr. Gilbert," I said. "He was nice. Always asked us about our school work and sometimes he would have us go to the store for him and tell us to buy what we wanted. Man, he was good people."

"Yeah, he was," Stone said. "He was my cousin."

"Mr. Gilbert was your cousin?" I asked stupidly. As soon as the question came out of my mouth, I know it was stupid to repeat what Stone had just said.

"Anyway, Pumpkin, I lost my mind. I had never seen your mom that distraught and she had reason to be. But after she left for Chicago, I went hunting for the men who hurt your mom and killed Gilbert, and for the men who originally hired me to do the job. Along with Stone, we found the men but not before we killed three other guys. And since I was still so pissed, when we found those assholes, I put at least six bullets in all of them.

"Then we went to the home of the guy who hired me. Come to find out his partner was his wife and she was the one who called all of the shots. So I killed them both."

Everything went quiet. No one said anything. My father looked down at the table again, Stone poured himself another cup of coffee and I just looked back and forth at both men. That was an unbelievable story. However, it wasn't the ending. I knew that. It couldn't be.

When he lifted his head, he finished the story. "I shot the woman in the head," he said. "She wanted to negotiate. She wanted to give me money." He smirked. "Can you believe that shit . . . they assault my wife and want to give me money." He shook his head. "I shot that stupid bitch in her head. And then her dumbass husband pleaded for his life and I emptied my chamber in his ass. And after that, I gave up guns."

"What the fuck?" We all turned and saw Damian standing in the kitchen doorway.

What the fuck was right.

INTERNATIONALLY KNOWN:
NEW YORK'S FINEST (PART 2)

KIKI SWINSON

Damian's Reality

I was bugging when I walked into the kitchen and saw Stone sitting at the table. This was some crazy, Twilight Zone shit. This motherfucker was worse than a cat with nine lives. Growing up I, and many others, had heard all of the stories about Big Stone escaping one misadventure after another one. I remember one time hearing about some guys sneaking into his house and surprising him in his bathtub. Somehow, they all ended up dead on his bathroom floor or in the hallway.

I was happy to see the old man. He looked down. He told us a little bit about his time in the Caribbean and hooking up with his doctor here, who took care of his burn wounds and patched him up. He left the area and wanted everyone to think he was dead, so he could rest and relax for a little while. Evidently, Foxx had taken control of his business ventures while he was gone.

We bullshitted for a little while. It was nice catching up on Stone's time on the island and he was equally impressed by everything we had done. He voiced his displeasure at us kidnapping innocent kids and involving family members. I didn't hear the story, but evidently Naomi's mom was an innocent victim of some crazy shit happening that didn't involve her. I now understood why Foxx wasn't crazy about my ideal. Hell, I felt low now. I was improvising, acting spontaneous.

However, Foxx vouched for me. He wanted his son back and he told Stone he was glad I stepped up. He gave me credit for making Naomi step up to the plate as well. He said me taking control and coming up with a spontaneous plan made Naomi realize she had to take responsibility and be accountable.

Naomi was smiling when Foxx was talking. She had my back as well. Stone talked about us being a team and how important that was. Not to mention, he gave me props for reviving the old Foxx. As he stated, "Digging the old man up from the grave." Naomi would later tell me about why Foxx had given up guns. She also shared that Foxx used to be a helluva shot just like Stone. I was amazed at this fucking family, and more amazed at the lives of both Stone and Foxx.

After we ate breakfast and took showers, Stone informed us to get our shit together, we were going back to Teaneck, to the house we had abandoned. When we tried objecting, he cut us off and informed us that the package was for one of his neighbors and we overreacted. He said it was no big deal, but if it was him, then he would have done the same thing.

When we arrived at the house in Teaneck, I was ready to turn back around when I saw the two black Chevy Tahoes in the driveway. But we parked the cars and took everything in. When we were situated in the house, Foxx and Stone went out again in separate cars. They returned again within ten minutes in one car.

After that, we chilled most of the day. Then around eight that night, Foxx said strap up. Naomi and I looked at each other. We didn't have a clue what was going on. So I asked the question.

"What's up, what's going on?

"It's game time, time to go to battle," Foxx said. "Be ready in thirty minutes."

I was lost, but that shit beat us staying in the house not doing shit but going stir crazy. Naomi and I rushed upstairs and got our shit together, which included putting on comfortable clothes. For us, that meant camouflage pants and jungle type boots along with a tee shirt and light jacket. The jacket was required to hide the ammo belts and shoulder holsters we had on. We all talked earlier and Stone told us that our arsenal for battle would include a Glock 27 and 40, along with the two Taser guns, to please Foxx he said, and M-4A1 assault rifles for close combat operations. I had never used this type of assault rifle before and I loved the AR-15, but Stone assured us that this was the shit and the way to go for what we were about to deal with.

Naomi and I didn't say shit. Stone had two other bags of weapons as well. He gave us both a KA-BAR combat knife. I could only speculate that whatever we were doing, it was some close quarters shit. So we were ready for whatever shit we were getting into.

We were ready to kick some ass when Stone told us to join him and Foxx in the kitchen. We all sat around the table. I think Naomi's and mine adrenaline was pumping. We wanted to kick some ass. Whose ass, we didn't have a clue. But it was time for action. I looked at Naomi and she was as anxious as a crack whore dying for a hit.

"Ok, it's time for you guys to reclaim your rightful place at the top of the game," Stone began. "We are attacking Pretty Pedro's and D.D's operations tonight." Stone looked at us and we both had stoic expressions on our faces. I think internally we both were happy. I know I was happy.

"Since Pedro and Dante' somewhat joined forces with Miguel Chavez, it's time for us to send a message. And that message is simple, you don't fuck with us." Stone paused, probably checking to see if he would get some kind of comment from Naomi or me, but we were cool. "Damian, you and Naomi will take one team—"

"One team?" both Naomi and I interrupted at the same time.

"Yeah, one team," Stone clarified. "I have four men outside waiting on us in the driveway. Two of those guys will go with you guys, the other two with Foxx and me. Your team, Damian, will hit the Butler Sky Rises. My team will hit Pedro's operation. We are not trying to steal anything or kidnap anyone." He looked at me when he said that. "This is about maiming and killing everyone that crosses our path. Plain and simple. It's time for us to send a message to let

Miguel know that we are coming for his ass! And we aren't trying to surprise him. I want him to know that it's not just three people he is dealing with, but a team."

"That shit won't matter," I stated. "We already know he is coming to insist on us coming alone as well as probably without weapons."

"Yeah, I know that. And we will deal with that when the time comes."

I shrugged my shoulders and listened as Stone told us his plan. The shit really was easy. Just go and start some shit. I told him I wanted to take out D.D. and he looked at me. Then he stated, "If you have your reasons, do what you have to do."

We didn't talk on our way to Queens. Stone's men were around our age. Both were black and physically fit. One looked like he pumped iron seven days a week. He was short and stocky, with muscles everywhere. I wondered if he was on steroids. His partner was a medium built guy like me. He was a light-skinned nigga who seemed to be pretty cool. When Naomi saw him, her eyes lit up and she said, "Junior."

He smiled back and said, "In the flesh."

Evidently, he was Stone's youngest son. I didn't know how many kids or sons Stone had, but Naomi seemed very familiar with Junior. That shit didn't bother me though. That shit between them was about business and from the silence in the car everyone knew that.

When we arrived at the BSRs, we parked where Foxx had parked when we were conducting surveillance. We needed to know what was up. Stone had told us that Dante would be in BSR #2 fucking around with a babe named Monica. Stone had coordinated with some cats from the utility company that was going to shut power to Pedro's and Dante's places in Harlem and Queen. So our game plan was to come in the building and do our damage. For us, this may be somewhat easier than Stone and Foxx's task of taking out Pedro. Reason being, Monica's place was on the first floor.

We had a synchronized time of eleven thirty that night for the power to be shutoff. I didn't need to see the utilities guy. As long as he did his job, we were cool. We were in place. Power Man was with me and Junior was with Naomi. Just like we did before, we all had throwaway phones with Bluetooth technology and were on the same conference call. There was light in the hallway of the first floor of BSR #2. As soon as the power was cut, we put on our night vision goggles and came in blazing from both sides. Dante had learned since we snatched his child. He had six men in the hallway and we took out all six. The night vision goggles made a huge difference.

Power Man and Junior went back outside. Each man taking an end of the building, just in case someone came to the aid of those we had taken out. Everything we had to do had to be precise and quick. Stone told us he heard the FBI had been lurking around some of the known drug spots throughout the five boroughs. So Naomi and I made our way to Room 106 in the middle of the hallway. I immediately kicked in the door and moved out the way, which was smart since gunshots came my way fast. I was lucky to get out of the way.

Naomi threw in the flash bang grenade and the high-powered flash and powerful bang did its job. Naomi had my back as I rushed in and saw Dante Daniels, aka D.D., hiding behind the sofa. I wanted so bad to talk shit, but I did what I came to do. We were on a schedule and we took care of business. For me, taking care of business meant one thing: a shot to the head and three shots to the body of bitch ass Dante'.

I told my guys to wrap it up and we busted ass getting back to the SUV. Our business was done. We were in and out in less than three minutes.

We wanted to send Miguel a message. If Stone and Foxx's operation was just as successful as our operation was, message was sent.

It was on.

INTERNATIONALLY KNOWN:
NEW YORK'S FINEST (PART 2)

KIKI SWINSON

Naomi's World of Crazy

When I was in Memphis, my recurring thought was of being a flight attendant. I missed flying, I missed jumping on planes and traveling all over the United States. I never thought much about being a flight attendant while I was doing it. I never thought I would miss that fucking job. However, in Memphis, I did. I missed flying the friendly skies.

Both operations went well. Stone and Foxx did their thing. Evidently, they killed Pedro, just like we killed D.D. It was a good night. I think both Damian and I were going through an adrenaline overdose. The excitement was thrilling. I think we were living for the excitement, looking forward to the next adventure. There was no doubt we loved the newfound danger in our lives.

I also think it was why we slept until noon the next day. We would have slept longer if it wasn't for the loud knocking at our bedroom door.

"Both of you, get your asses up," my dad said. "We have a phone call in ten minutes, you guys need to be downstairs in the kitchen."

"Okay," I said weakly.

"Okay, then get your asses up," he stated as he walked away.

I struggled to get up, but Damian ran to the bathroom. That early morning piss was probably kicking his ass. I trudged myself to the bathroom and washed my face. I even grabbed my toothbrush and brushed my teeth. I slipped on something comfortable and grabbed my housecoat. Damian said he needed to take a dump. The phone call sounded important. If it involved Reggie or my mom, I wanted to be there.

When I reached the kitchen, Stone and my father were sitting at the kitchen table with a cell phone sitting in the middle of the table. As soon as I sat down, he hit the Send button on the cell phone.

"Wait, we need to wait on Damian," I protested.

"No, we need to handle business," my dad said. "If he's not here, that means we need to back brief him."

"I told you, don't call me, I will call you!" Miguel Chavez said in perfect English. Not like his father, who had a heavy Mexican accent, although his English was pretty good. "You want Reggie alive, you do as I say. You give me respect and pay attention to my demands."

"Chavez, shut the fuck up and listen," my father said surprisingly. "You have someone who shares my blood. You wanted us to lie down and die, so you can justify killing Reggie to your dad. I know Marco is vacationing in Brazil. He is off the grid for another week. Last night was about letting you know that we are not laying down. If you want your money, it's time to trade. If not, kill Reggie and let's start the war."

The phone was silent. Absolute silence. I assumed the young asshole was trying to figure out his next move. I was scratching my head. I had never seen this Foxx before. He was supposed to be a burglar, a thief, but the man was strong, powerful. I think he went out of his way to keep Reggie and I in the dark about who the real man was.

"Mr. Foxx, that's a bold move on your part," Miguel finally stated. "Reggie disrespected me. My dad would understand."

"No, son, he won't," my dad replied. "Miguel, it's arithmetic, simple math. You kill Reggie. Cool. But guess what, we will hunt you and your men down. First, your father loses a son, plus twenty or thirty good men. Secondly and more important than your death or the deaths of your men, he loses millions in revenue. That's the bottom line, son. You are about to put five million dollars in your pocket. That's five million you didn't have before. A four million dollar profit."

I looked at my father and asked myself what in the hell was he talking about? First, he was playing with Reggie's life, and now he was talking math and numbers, and a four million dollar profit. What in the fuck was up with this?

"Old man, you are delusional," Miguel responded weakly. There was no confidence in his voice. I was completely lost. I didn't understand shit that was going on. I looked at Stone and his expression didn't tell me anything.

"Son, I have sources just like you have sources," my dad stated. His tone was full of confidence and truthfully, full of arrogance. But he was clearly the one in control. At that moment, Stone put his finger to his lips and I turned around to see Damian's facial expression.

"My sources told me that the shipment the FBI and DEA retrieved only had a street value of maybe one to one and a half million dollars. Hell, the operation wasn't even worth their time. You played Reggie's wife, Vanessa, to make that bogus ass phone call. And you knew those dumbasses at the FBI would jump on it because it was about making career changes. You set all of this shit up and it backfired on you. You never expected the other dealers to unite and Reggie staying in the area and selling his old shit fucked up your game and more importantly, fucked up your profit margin."

Once again, the phone went silent. I could sense Miguel was grinding his teeth. From where we stood, we had that bastard by the balls. Miguel was a fucking pussy. He was dumbass nigga with dreams of taking over his father's enterprise. He was a little boy trying to play a man's game and our operation had to suffer for his bullshit. My father was spewing out shit I never knew. And looking at Damian, he was completely taken by surprise as well.

Who was this man talking shit like this was his world? I didn't recognize my father in this role. Or maybe I did. When I thought about the times going shooting with him and Stone, elements of this man came out. He had confidence and he and Uncle Stone used to talk a lot of shit to each other. And I do remember when my mom just got up and left for Chicago. It changed my father. It was as if he became a different man. He was more laid back. And it was as if his give a damn factor had disappeared. Now it took his only son being kidnapped to stir up the old man. And truth be told, I loved this Foxx. I think both Reggie and I got it honestly. We were his kids. And in this case, the apples didn't fall too far from the tree.

"Well, Mr. Foxx, what are you recommending?" Miguel finally asked. Tone and voice strength mean something. I don't think Miguel Chavez realized that. The man sounded weak and all of a sudden—afraid. Hell, I wasn't in his shoes, but listening to my father, I felt afraid.

"I want my son back, you want your five million," he began. "Let's make this happen. Let's do the right thing. Even trade, Reggie for five mil and there's no hard feelings. Business is business. You win. We don't discuss again and we don't let this affect Reggie and Marco's relationship. You may not realize it, but Marco needs Reggie, Miguel. If he didn't, you would have asked his permission to do what you are doing. Let's end this shit now."

I saw my dad's eyes. He was blowing smoke up Miguel's ass big time. He knew, like we all knew, this shit was not over. Maybe it was just a feeling I was having, but someone was going to die. And I knew that someone could be any one of us at the table now, or Reggie, or even that asshole Miguel. But if this didn't go right, our lives would be changed. And it wouldn't be for the best.

"You are definitely asking for a lot, old man," Miguel said in return. "How do you know my father didn't sanction this himself? He's a very powerful man and when he wants something, he gets it."

"Miguel, don't waste my time with your rubbish. Time is of the essence. And we have scores to settle. I have your money and you have my son. Now where will it be?" my father immediately retorted.

I was impressed with my father's logic. He kept bringing it back to the money. That's why we were in this crazy ass business, to get paid.

"Are you prepared to take him anyway you get 'em?" Miguel asked. The sound of his comment shocked me. And suddenly, we weren't sure if Reggie was even alive. We needed proof of life before we set up the meeting place.

I jumped in before my dad could reply. "Miguel," I said calmly. "We want proof of life." My father looked at me and it wasn't a good look. I glanced over at Uncle Stone and although his expression hadn't changed, I could tell he was a little disturbed by my statement.

"Proof of life?" Miguel said. "And I thought we were working on an element of faith."

Hearing Miguel give my father the run around about Reggie made me so upset with myself for blurting out those words. Damn! I fucked up! His statement was spoken with confidence. Had I awakened the sleeping dog?

"We will do this tonight." Miguel finally agreed. "I will get back with you about the time and place. And as far as proof of life, as soon as we hang up the phone I will send you your proof of life."

"Miguel, remember the clock is ticking," my father stated.

"I realize that. And so that we're clear, I want your precious little girl to be the bag lady tonight," Miguel commented. "And if anyone else shows up, then your son will be a dead man. It's just that simple." He continued and then the phone went dead.

As soon as the phone went dead, I had to ask the question, "Did I fuck that up?"

"Nothing we can't recover from," Stone said as he got up from the table.

"Yeah, you fucked up," my dad said differently. We looked at each other. His gaze was hardened. I could tell how livid he'd become over my outburst. His tone and demeanor had changed. And I knew it would take him some time to get over it.

"This was a negotiation between two people, Pumpkin—a seasoned veteran who knows the law of the land . . . and a boy who wants to be a man, and impress his father. I broke that down for young Miguel. It was a matter of him trusting me. Then your interference broke him out of that trance I had put him in. I wanted him to have a certain mindset. You destroyed the trust he suddenly had in me and took away our advantage."

"Dad, I'm sorry," I said with conviction. "It sounded to me that he didn't have a plan on us meeting. And if he didn't, how do we know Reggie is still alive."

As soon as the words came out of my mouth, the phone beeped. It was a video of Reggie tied up in a chair. A newspaper was in front of him with the time in big red letters. The video was only twenty seconds long. Five seconds in, a voice said, "Here's your proof of life." It was Miguel's voice, but he wasn't in the picture. I looked at Reggie, as we all did, and noticed he had been beaten.

I felt tears well up in my eyes. Now I really wanted to kill the motherfucker. This shit was personal. And the only thing I could wonder was what was up with this crazy ass, punk bitch motherfucker. We had a good thing going. His father had a good thing going. And now he was tripping. He had his own agenda and we were paying for it.

"Damian, get the laptop out of the living room," Stone said.

"There is your proof of life," my father said to me. I looked at him again. Truthfully, I hadn't seen my dad this pissed off at me in a very long time. "How do you feel seeing Reggie like this? You want to kill Miguel now? You want some kind of revenge?"

The answers to all of those questions were yes, and why wouldn't they be yes. I didn't say anything to my dad's stupid ass questions.

Damian brought the laptop in and sat it on the table, along with the computer bag. Stone swung it around and got a USB cord out and hooked up the phone to the laptop and started tapping keys on the laptop. He worked in silence. No one said anything. The whole time my father's eyes were still on me. I played it off. I was in the wrong. I knew that. I was in a world of crazy. I knew it from the start. I knew it now.

After Stone was through, we all stood behind him. He had blown up the video of Reggie. This was crazy, like my dream of me being some warrior bitch. Reggie really was sitting in a chair in a warehouse. What we saw was a part of the warehouse that Stone had blown up. It was behind Reggie. It was a sign on the back wall of the warehouse. The sign said *Genesis Antiques and Things*.

"We got you motherfucker," Stone said with a smile in his voice.

We live in a world of crazy.

INTERNATIONALLY KNOWN: NEW YORK'S FINEST (PART 2)

KIKI SWINSON

Damian Must Prove Himself

I walked in on the middle of the phone call to Miguel Chavez. I initially thought this was a family thing and I had been excluded. But it wasn't anything like it. Foxx was about taking care of business and trying to get his son back. I felt bad for him. Naomi was a daddy's girl to her heart and Foxx coming down on her was a downer. After Stone told us he knew where the warehouse was located, he recommended we go upstairs and jump in the shower and get ourselves together.

I wasn't mad at anyone. But I could tell Naomi wasn't in the greatest of moods. She, just like me, had seen a side of Foxx we never knew about. We had known the man as a laid back dad and all around good guy. Now we were seeing another side of him and he couldn't understand our concerns.

Foxx grabbed a beer and went outside through the back door. We made our way upstairs. We had just gotten out of the shower and put clothes on when Stone knocked on the door.

INTERNATIONALLY KNOWN

"What's up Stone?" I asked when he opened the bedroom door.

"We need to talk," he said to us. "You need to know about your dad, once and for all." He was looking at Naomi and I understood. I was about to walk out the room without saying a word, when Stone stopped me and told me to sit down as well.

He sat in the big recliner chair in the big bedroom. He leaned forward and if he saw what I saw in Naomi's eyes, he knew she was hurt. She was Reggie's business partner, plus, she was his sister. She was naturally upset.

"Long ago, Naomi, your father and I had our own little business together. We did whatever jobs came our way. And the most lucrative jobs we ever had was hostage negotiation or retrieval."

Stone stopped talking and I was glad he did. But wait; did you say hostage negotiations or retrievals? What the fuck? Who in the hell were these two guys? They had been in our lives forever and today was the first time we were hearing about this. My initial thought was did Reggie know about this shit. If anyone did, it was probably him. Foxx and Reggie had always had that bond that they talked a lot. I know Foxx wanted to school Reggie on the ways of handling business in the streets. It was definitely different from handling business in a boardroom, business building or on Wall Street.

"That's why Foxx took the lead on procuring Reggie back," Stone continued. "You see, Naomi, we have lived this world. We were the best at it. Your

dad always portrayed the life of a petty thief or burglar, because it was about ensuring his wife and kids
were safety. What we did, we did on the low because
we pissed a lot of folks off."

"Stone, I don't believe this shit," Naomi objected. "If you guys did stuff like this, we would have
known. Mom would have known, me and Reggie
would have known." Naomi suddenly stopped talking.
She was looking at Stone. For whatever reason, she
could sense he was holding something back. For the
life of me, I didn't get it. The man's expression never
changed. It was just as stoic as it was when he waltzed
into the room. But she knew something wasn't right.

"Uncle Stone, no way you're telling me mom
knew about this?" Stone didn't reply. "Shit, did Reggie know about this too?"

"Yeah, he did," Stone confirmed my suspicions
and probably Naomi's as well. This was pretty fucked
up. I understood me not knowing, I wasn't family, but
Naomi. That was just wrong.

"It was for your safety," Stone said. "Plus, this
wasn't something we were shouting from the highest
rooftop. People who needed our services usually got
our information from others. Mostly by asking
around."

"How long did y'all do this?" I asked.

"Probably for a good seven or eight years," Stone
responded immediately. "Before you ask, I will give
you a very quick history of how we got into this. Years
ago, a drug dealer named Dicky Red was into kidnapping family members of his rivals in the business.

INTERNATIONALLY KNOWN

Well, one day he snatched the daughter of one of the guys we used to roll with named Johnson. Johnson hired us to get his kid back. We did the do. We tried to do it without bloodshed, but I think both Foxx and I knew we had to take Red out. If we didn't, he would keep doing the shit he was doing.

"From there, our reputation grew . . . or, maybe I should say, my reputation grew. Your dad set it up that I was the front man and I was the one with the reputation. I had family, but no one knew anything about me. I was the mysterious one. But truthfully, your dad was the one working behind the scenes. He was the brain of any operation we did. He did the hard thinking and I was the enforcer. Although he was just as good a shooter as I was, he preferred to do things with talking versus just strong arming and shooting up places. But when the situation called for it, he did his part."

"Stone, that's not my dad, that's not Foxx," Naomi objected again.

Stone got up from the recliner and sat next to her. He hugged her with one arm and pulled her to him and kissed her on the head. "Yeah, Pumpkin, that's your dad. He taught Reggie a lot of what he knows. You know Foxx can talk the ear off a dead person and that son-of-a-bitch is the best damn negotiator I have ever seen, and believe me, I have seen my share of smooth talkers."

I was completely stunned. Foxx? This shit was unbelievable. No wonder Reggie could start doing the shit he was doing way back in high school. He would always talk shit about doing something this way or that way. Me and the boys would listen because Reggie really sounded like he was ten or fifteen years older than what he really was. He would amaze us with his shit. Now I knew, it was all Foxx, his dad, who told him shit about how to manipulate in this fucking business.

"Why did you guys stop?" Naomi asked.

"Not my choice," Stone replied. "It was your daddy. When they assaulted your mom and she decided to go to Chicago, he decided to get out. After all, your mother didn't give him a choice. It was either he get out of the business or she would leave him forever. The only thing, he wouldn't allow her to take you guys. But after she was gone, he missed her. She was and still is the love of his life."

I tried not to think of my family dynamics. I wished my father was around and my mother was a loving mother. I didn't have that luxury. My shit was whacked out typical ghetto bullshit. A dad who came around to fuck mom or better yet, to get his rocks off, and a young mom who was more worried about partying than raising a son.

I always envied the times Reggie would tell me about Foxx telling him this or telling him that. That motherfucker had it good and even today, I don't think he knows how good he really had it. Hell, he was the man he is today because of his dad and his mom. I think the unfortunate thing about Reggie was his head got too big. After all, Reggie started slinging drugs in high school and he had his own crew by the time we graduated high school. By the time we walked across the stage, we had already made an easy one hundred thousand in spending money.

This motherfucker had bitches we went to school with hooking for him and hell, young cats were selling drugs for him. He would always tell me, this was our shit together, but actually, Reggie was too selfish to share any damn thing. He wanted me to be his Stone, but from listening to the real Big Joey Stone, he and Foxx were not only the best of friends, they were equal partners. Reggie would never let anyone be equal to him . . . including his own sister, Naomi.

"Naomi, what your dad has been trying to teach you for years to be strong," Stone stated. He was still hugging his pseudo niece, trying to comfort her. In some ways, I guess he was giving her the compassionate comforting that I couldn't. My comforting consisted of hard dick and a snake-like tongue. That was probably best used later after he got Reggie back.

"Men like your father and I are used to teaching and telling you the things that will make you successful in life," he continued. "And we wouldn't tell you anything that would hurt you. Hell, we all know Reggie is in this mess because he is hardheaded and couldn't take a damn day off. Even with the Feds on his ass, he decided to stay and put himself in danger. Not realizing that he was also putting everyone else in danger.

"Now, we need you strong. Both you and Damian have proved that you guys are a formidable couple and could capture the world if you had to. The good thing is this time you guys have help from two old school fools who have captured the world a time or two. Learn from us."

I felt good to hear Stone mentioned my name. I know his conversation was about Naomi keeping her shit together, but he acknowledged that she and I were in this shit together. That meant something to me.

Naomi kissed Stone on the cheek and gave him a tight hug. He got up from the bed and was about to leave, when I stopped him.

"What's our next move?" I asked.

"Genesis Antiques and Things' warehouse is in the clothing district of Manhattan. I have a couple of my men checking out the place as we speak. Foxx and I think it is best to surprise them tonight. We are waiting to hear from Miguel, but I think we will have a little surprise of our own for the young Chavez."

You couldn't help but love Stone. He was direct and told you what you needed to know. It wasn't always what you wanted to hear. He really was a mover and shaker, and he made shit happen.

"Do you think they will move him or that it may be a set-up?" I weighed in. "It may be he wanted us to see the sign."

"Yeah, I thought about that, until I looked at the video maybe another four or five times," Stone answered. "I don't think they realized they got the shot in the camera. The sign was on the very top of the video feed and I think whoever took the video, just shot the damn thing, not really thinking of quality or background."

INTERNATIONALLY KNOWN

"So what do we do in the meantime," Naomi asked.

"For now, just chill."

"Cool," I said.

"Matter of fact, your dad is putting together a huge meal," Stone mentioned. "I think his crazy ass is fixing burritos, refried beans, enchiladas, tamales and any other Mexican dish he can throw together."

Both Naomi and I laughed. "Yeah, that's Foxx," Naomi said. "Whenever he is hard at thinking or trying to solve a problem, he cooks his ass off. And the ironic thing is that shit be good. Don't know who taught his ass how to cook, but they did a damn good thing."

We all smiled. Now it was about waiting out the craziness, and being patient when you were anxious as hell was the hardest thing to do in the world at that moment.

And patience in this case was not a virtue.

INTERNATIONALLY KNOWN: NEW YORK'S FINEST (PART 2)

KIKI SWINSON

Mayhem in Manhattan

After Stone talked to Damian and I, I thought about the time when my mom left us and temporarily moved to Chicago. Reggie and I always thought it was just a visit to her sister. I laughed to myself. I mentioned Reggie and I knew that motherfucker probably knew everything that was going on. Knowing Foxx as I did, I was sure Reggie was the one person who told everything he was doing. Just in case shit didn't work out right, Reggie would be the breadwinner.

My father was always the number one man in my life, even more than Reggie. During that time when mom left, he stepped up and did his thing as a parent. He made sure we got to school, cooked, washed and cleaned. Shit, he even helped us with our homework. When I think of my father as a young man, a young dad, I remember the times he stayed in both of our shit to make sure we did the right thing when it came to school and everything else. If we started something like sports, gymnastics, karate, we couldn't quit.

We had to complete what we started. And that's what we were doing now, finishing what we started. I could only hope and pray it came out in our favor.

My father had outdone himself on dinner. I actually had come down to help him. I kissed him on the cheek as I entered the kitchen and he gave me a quick hug and kissed me on the forehead. We didn't talk as we worked in the kitchen. He had thoughts on his mind just like I did. We just did our thing.

Watching my dad work in the kitchen brought back a lot of wonderful, but sad memories for me. They were good memories when we created them years ago. Both Reggie and I missed our mom, but we knew she was only visiting. Or so we thought. At least I didn't know all of the dynamics going on. But one of the things we did as a family was cook and clean house. And when we attacked the kitchen, it was as we were doing now, hit an area and press on. Everything was synchronized as if we had orchestrated some kind of kitchen work detail. Then it was the three of us, now it was only my dad and me. That's why I was sad. Reggie was the third member of this team. I missed him and so did my dad. I knew he wanted his son back. Shit, I wanted my brother back.

And I hoped we could cook together one last time.

Why we never did this with our mom, I couldn't tell you. Maybe it was just a thing between father and his two kids. Maybe. Maybe mom didn't need the help. I laughed to myself because I knew my father didn't need the help.

I wanted to say we ate in silence, but that would be the farthest thing from the truth. Stone and my father actually did some serious reminiscing about when they were a team of hostage negotiators and retrievals. Some of the stories they told were crazy as hell. I couldn't believe my father did that crazy as shit. Plus, the thing that really got to me and I was so glad I could witness it was the way dad's eyes lit up as they told their stories.

I loved my father. He really was my hero. But I looked at him in a different light today. Since coming back from Memphis, he had surprised me every damn day with something he had done. He had taken control like I had never seen him take control before. He had talked shit like I had never seen or heard him before. He had put his dick on his shoulder and double dared Miguel or anyone else to knock it off.

I loved the stories because it taught me more about my dad and Big Stone. They were a mess together. It was about living and making sure others lived as well. I never saw my father as the H-N-I-C like Stone but they sounded like they were equal in every sense of the word. Then they got serious and got it back to the here and now.

"I think we should mimic the Hopkins heist," my father said.

Stone was no longer laughing and smiling. "I think you are right," he said stoically.

"What was the Hopkins heist?" Damian asked.

"This black businessman named George Hopkins' daughter had been kidnapped," my father began. "Hopkins did a lot of business in the black neighborhoods."

"I remember the Hopkins buildings and projects in East New York," I said.

"Yeah, George owned those buildings," Stone volunteered.

"Yeah, he did," my dad said. "But did you hear about a gang who called themselves the ENY Bandits broke into George's house and raped and killed his wife and kidnapped his teenage daughter? They wanted a million dollars in ransom money. We found out they were holding her in a small warehouse in East New York. This wasn't about negotiating and we didn't want to negotiate. This was about death and retrieval."

My dad looked at me and I returned his glare. I knew he was talking directly to me now. "George gave us the money and we set up the buy. The game plan was for me to go in the warehouse . . . by myself . . . hand over the money and I got the girl back. But we knew the Bandits. They were sure as shit going to kill us both. So we decided to say fuck it."

"Yeah, fuck it," Stone intervened. This was crazy the way both of them were telling the story without missing a beat. "We drunk a fifth of Tequila and got our own little gang together. We sat down in this very house we are in today and set up a strategy. We figured one person would have a gun on the girl. Our game plan was crazy as hell. It was eight of us. We knew the Bandits had at least twenty to thirty members and we didn't know how many would be there."

"So we just said fuck it and decided we would walk in with the money," my dad jumped in. "And told the Bandits we have their money and we want the girl. Also, we wouldn't pay any attention to what they had to say. Just walk in the front door and keep on walking until we were at least ten or fifteen feet in front of them. And guess what? That's exactly what we did."

"But that wasn't the crazy shit," Stone continued. "Your dad walked five feet in front of us, bent down and showed the Bandits the money. The leader told him to slide the money over and he said no. Told him to come and get the money. At first, he was hesitant and tried to send one of his men. But Foxx told him no, only him. When he came over, Foxx told him that I had my rifle trained on his head, and another one of our guys had his rifle trained on the guy who was holding the gun to the girl's head. And if anything went wrong, they were the first to die. Then he told him to let the girl go now, while they were making the exchange."

"And when he said no," he picked it up. "Stone shot him in the head and our other guy shot the guy holding the girl in the head as well. And you would think all hell would break out, but it didn't. I think everyone was in shock. We quickly told the other fifteen or so gang members that they could have the money and no one else had to die. And guess what, they went for it."

Damian and I looked at each other, both of us saying, "Who are these damn fools?" By all rights, I thought he and Stone should probably be dead by now. How they lived this long was beyond me.

INTERNATIONALLY KNOWN

Finally he and Stone then began to tell us the plan. We were going to bust into the place the same way. It was going to be six of us walking through the front door. The only exception was Stone would have another six men coming in from the top of the warehouse, three on each side. His gun would be aimed at Miguel, while my father's gun would be aimed at the nigga who would had Reggie.

Damian had mentioned that we were seven hundred seventy-five thousand dollars short. Stone had evidently given us the money. The whole game plan was predicated on Miguel. I would be the one walking up front once we stopped and opening the oversized duffel bag with five million dollars in it. My job was simple, tell Miguel the same thing my dad had tried to tell the ENY Bandit leader years ago. And truthfully, we all hoped it would be different results. As in, Miguel would accept the money and keep it moving. If he didn't, death was definitely the outcome. Maybe death for all of us. Who knew?

Stone had predicted Miguel would call late, around midnight or so. His two guys were still casing the warehouse. From what one of Stone's men told him, the warehouse district was busy and several warehouses had round-the-clock operations. The Genesis's warehouse was one of two warehouses they owned. This particular one was for storage. The business was actually owned by a friend of Marco Chavez, who let the son use it for several days to keep Reggie kidnapped. I was sure he had used it before for other crazy ass shit like this.

The warehouse was one of the smaller warehouses in the clothing district. Although clothes and clothing material were the primary items stored in the district, the name was misleading. Other industries had warehouses in the area as well. Genesis's smaller warehouse sat between two bigger warehouses.

From the photographs Stone had received from his men, Reggie was sitting right smack in the middle of the warehouse. There were four men watching him. They stated that if we got there before hand, we could probably take Reggie with only these four guys getting killed.

My dad and Stone liked that game plan. That was Plan B to the Plan A they had already come up with. It was nine o'clock on a Friday night. The good thing was many of the warehouses didn't have a weekend shift. Since the recession, many companies had cut back big on those type expenses. Come ten, eleven or midnight, many workers were going home to enjoy the weekend.

So Plan B was put into motion unless we heard from Miguel while we were en route.

We were meeting Stone's men a couple of miles from the warehouse district. The four of us had filed into one of the black SUVs and Stone was driving with Damian in the passenger seat. My father and I were in the back seat.

"You good?" my father asked me out of the blue.

"Yeah, I'm doing good," I replied. Truthfully, I had big time butterflies in my stomach. Although we had been kicking ass and doing all kinds of spontaneous, off the wall shit, this was it. This was the actual rescue and if anything went wrong, Reggie could die. Truthfully speaking, all of us could die.

"Well, to let you guys know," my father started his conversation. "The Feds got a rumor that you guys would be in Brooklyn and Bedford-Stuy tonight gunning for drug dealers."

"What?" I said out of shock. "How you know that?"

"Because we called the rumor in," Stone said. "One, it keeps them off your trail and two, it also buys you time to figure out what you guys want to do after this."

"What you mean, buy us time?" I asked.

"I think it's finally time for us to pull roots and get out of here," my dad said. "At least for your mom and me. I hope you, Reggie and Damian decide to do the same thing. Believe me, after tonight, if all doesn't go well, we may all be hunted prey for the Chavez family. As a matter of fact, if it goes well, we may still be hunted."

"Why you say that, dad?"

"Because, even though this wasn't sanctioned by Marco, Miguel is his son and what he did was disrespectful to Marco. But what we are about to do to Miguel will be downright insulting and embarrassing, especially in front of his men, who he's supposed to be leading. Marco wouldn't have a choice but to make an example of us. Or at least try to make an example out of us."

I actually had never thought about that shit. It made sense though and that's what really scared me. I used to fuck Marco, now I had to worry about this little dick as nigga trying to kill me and my family. And I wasn't having that. Now way. Fuck that! This whole thing was crazy. And as much as I wanted to hug and kiss my brother, I also wanted to kick his ass for not leaving New York. How dare he put us through all of this bullshit! All of this shit could've been avoided a long time ago.

"You think the Feds bought the rumor?" Damian asked.

"Yeah," my dad responded. "Evidently you guys have a couple of lead agents at the FBI and DEA who are hot for you guys. I was told that for the first couple of months you guys were missing, the Feds had undercover agents sticking around several hoods trying to catch you three."

"Seriously," I said.

"Yeah, seriously," he replied. "So it was easy throwing those carrots out there and let them chase it."

Stone went over both Plan A and Plan B in details. This was about doing everything right. One bad move and Reggie could be dead. We had to be flawless in our execution. I thought we were ready and prepared for anything.

When we met at the rendezvous spot, Stone gave us all one last briefing. It was ten-thirty and we still hadn't heard from Miguel yet. When Stone talked to his man at the warehouse, he said there was now seven men at the warehouse and they all were just milling around the place. Three or four of them were playing dominoes and the others were just fucking around trying to keep busy.

So we did our thing. We had three SUVs and parked them between warehouse alleyways within a block or so of our destination. Then we moved on feet, strapped with guns and rifles. Although the warehouse was smaller than the others, it still had two passenger doors to walk through. There was also a bigger warehouse house to drive trucks and heavy equipment through but it was closed, and there was no sense in us trying to open the big door and alerting Miguel's guys that the cavalry had arrived.

We still had six people going through the two doors, three on each side. And just like Plan A, we still had the other six guys come down from the top. However, the six was now eight with Stone's other two guys who were already at the warehouse. When we burst through the doors we really did catch the kidnappers by surprise. Three tried to pick up the weapons but Stone and my father handled their business and took them out.

No lie. I don't know how in the hell they were that accurate from that range, but both had one shot kill shots. And I don't know which one of them did it, but one of them took out two guys. What the fuck? My dad and uncle were lethal, and crazy as a motherfucker.

The other guys gave up without a fight. Several of Stone's men went and got their weapons and tied them up.

"Hey, fool," I said to Reggie before I attempted to untie him.

"Hey, yourself," he replied. We looked at each other. He was beaten and bruised. But what was more devastating was that his pride was hurt. I could see it in his eyes. I so wanted to give him a hug, but I wanted to untie him first. But as much as I wanted to untie Reggie, we couldn't yet. Attached to the back of his chair was a bomb. "Let me guess, Miguel left a little surprise for you guys back there, right?"

I didn't say anything. My father, Stone and Damian came around the back of Reggie and took a look for themselves. "Shit," my dad said. "Whatcha' think?" he said to Stone.

"Man, I think I can defuse it," Stone said. "You know it's been a while since I done some shit like this, so I hope I don't blow us the fuck up." Stone smiled, a toothy smile. I n all of this fucking madness, I actually think Foxx and Stone were happy to work together again like they used to.

"What time is it?" Reggie asked.

"What, you have somewhere to go?" I joked.

"No, smartass," Reggie boomed. "I heard Miguel tell his men he and the other guys would be back around eleven and the massacre would be around one."

"Massacre?" I said in the form of a question.

"Yeah, massacre, sis," Reggie replied. "This was never meant to be an exchange. This little fuck is trying to make his bones and we are his patsies."

"How is it going, Stone?" my dad asked his best friend while looking at his watch.

INTERNATIONALLY KNOWN

"I just need another minute," Stone said.

As soon as the words came out of his mouth, the big double doors for truck entrances opened and a big truck was positioned for backing into the warehouse.

"Shit," was the only thing I remember my dad saying before all hell broke loose.

Bullets started flying all over the place. The truck was like a two-ton Army truck; with men jumping out the back with assault rifles like some shit you see in a military movie. Stone was shouting something and although I couldn't make out what it was, evidently Foxx understood. He got in front of Reggie on one knee returning fire. We were fortunate we had the other eight guys on the top level of the warehouse, because the six of us wouldn't have been able to handle the guys by ourselves. Plus, it was only five of us with Stone trying to defuse Reggie's bomb.

They had other guys running in from around the truck, which told me there was probably another truck parked outside. One of the guys on the floor was hit and then Damian was hit too. As much as I wanted to say something or do something for him, the best I could do was move in his direction to make sure he was okay.

The guys above us were handling their business because our enemies were falling like fucking flies. And then it happened.

Miguel came in shouting something and I don't know who made the shot but a bullet hit him squarely in the middle of his forehead and he stopped in his tracks.

KIKI SWINSON

And just like that, the shooting stopped. From both sides. They only had four guys standing. I knew it was at least twenty something guys lying on the floor or inside the bed of the two-ton truck dead . . . including one Miguel Chavez.

"Let's get out of here before the cops come," Stone said. The four guys who were still standing had dropped their weapons. Some of the guys who had been on the upper level had come down. They made sure the guys didn't have any more weapons and instead of killing them, my father told them to get the hell away from here and to never come back. And they indeed took off running.

Stone and my dad carried Reggie. He had an arm around each man. I took the lead with one of Stone's men and we moved with purpose. Damian was by me too. He was shot in the shoulder, but he was good. The other men were behind us and we were moving to get the hell out of there. One of the guys had already pulled a SUV up and he and another guy ran in the warehouse and grabbed their dead comrade.

Reggie was thrown in the back of the SUV we were driving. We all got in and hauled ass out of Manhattan. We all went in different directions. The funny thing was we didn't hear sirens until we were a good two or three miles away and they were moving in the other direction.

I was exhausted, but I felt good. It was the adrenaline that was kicking my ass. Stone was driving and I was his shotgun. My father was attending to both Reggie's and Damian's wounds. We weren't breaking any speed limits. It was all about getting back to Jersey safe and sound, and hopefully getting the fuck out of this whole fucking area as soon as possible. I wasn't sure if Damian or Reggie would be able to travel by tomorrow.

Stone pulled out his cell phone and called someone I assumed was a doctor because he told the person on the phone about Damian's and Reggie's injuries, and even told the caller where we were staying at.

If this wasn't the craziest shit then I don't know what was. And I truly didn't realize how crazy until I heard my dad on the phone telling my mother "Code DC." That was all he said. When I asked him what that meant, he told me that was his mother's signal to pack up the family and move to Denver, Colorado. It was their emergency code if shit got too crazy in New York, and he wanted her and her family to even move out of Chicago to a safer place. A place no one would even imagine looking. Their old friend, George Hopkins, lived in Denver.

What the fuck?!

It was then that I realized that Miguel Chavez was truly dead and we were responsible. And as crazy as it sounded, it was also then that I realized we weren't going anywhere. We were going to stand our ground and fight it out with Marco Chavez. We knew we were going to have to deal with him next. Marco wasn't going to let us rest without seeing one of us pay for what we did to his son, Miguel. So, we say, bring it on. We never found out if that UPS driver was a Fed or not. And it wouldn't surprise us to find out it was.

It also wouldn't surprise us to find out Miguel was behind the delivery driver incident. Mobsters like him always had a few tricks up their sleeves. Either way, a war was in the works and believe me, we will be ready. And as far as the Feds go, we feel like if we stay off the radar, we'd be okay. But if for some reason, we happened to run into them, then we'd rather go out like soldiers than to let them take us into custody. My family and I aren't built for the prison cells, so we're going to do everything we can to live on these streets until the day we all die. I know it sounds crazy. But hey, we lived by the gun and that's how we intend to die. That alone makes me and my family *New York's Finest.*

INTERNATIONALLY KNOWN

SNEAK PEEK AT

"CHEAPER TO KEEP HER
PART 4"
(AMERICA'S MOST WANTED)
IN STORES 12/18/2012

···

WHY ME?
CHAPTER ONE

While I lay in the hospital bed, Agent Sean had two new agents posted up outside my door standing guard. Having me to assist them in their investigation against Bishop and his crew, went directly out the window after I witnessed Chrissy execute Agent Morris and Agent Pax. I was officially a government witness and I hated it. Sean gave those other agents strict orders to protect me at all cost. That meant it was controlled traffic coming in and going out. So all my plans of getting the hell out of Newark, New Jersey and heading to another state to start my life over was a distant memory.

This morning marked my second day in this shit hole of a hospital. Not only was the accommodations whack, the food sucked too and I wanted out of here. The Indian doctor that was on duty assured me that I'd most likely be discharged within the week, which

KIKI SWINSON

meant he really didn't know. His accent alone irritated the hell out of me. And the fact that he wasn't the actual doctor who operated on me, made me question why he was here in the first place. I gritted my teeth at him after he gave me that lame ass answer and then I turned my attention towards the TV. There wasn't anything on worth watching, but it was more entertaining than listening to that bootleg ass doctor.

After he exited my room, I tried to get into the *Celebrity Apprentice* reality show but my mind wouldn't let me. I swear, I couldn't take my mind off Bishop and the fact that he sent Chrissy out to hunt me down and take me the fuck out. Who would've thought that he had an inside connection with a Special Agent? When I searched through Bishop's phone that night and called her back, I never would've thought that in a million years that I was talking to an agent. That ho really pulled the wool over my eyes. And so had Bishop. The whole time I thought she was another one of his fuck partners, trying to steal my spot. But no, that cold-hearted bitch was an assassin on a mission. So, I thank God for his protection because those two federal agents dropped the ball.

Aside from Chrissy, I realized that I was learning more and more about Bishop. That guy was well connected and when he had his mind fixed on something, he won't stop breathing until it was done. I just hoped that I'd be able to slip through the crack before he closed in on me. The only good thing that weighed in my favor was the fact that I wasn't the only person on his shit list. His main lady Keisha was at the top of his hit list, so if I used that to my advantage, then I may come out in the clear. I guess, time would tell though.

During the next several hours, nurses and CNA's paraded in and out of my room and I wanted them to stop. I pulled one of the CNA's to the side and asked her a few questions. She was a young, short, black chick with a head filled with blonde and black hair extensions. And when she opened her mouth to speak, I knew she was straight from the hood. "Is there any way I could request not to have any of the nurses to come in here for a while? All of this running in and out is preventing me from relaxing. I am about to go crazy."

She smiled. "It's hospital policy to check on da' patients around da' clock. Girl, if da' doctor found out we ain't been in here to check your vitals, our butts will be on the chopping block and I can't lose my job. It's bad enough dat' I don't get no child support from my baby daddies, so you know I gotta' follow da' rules."

"How long have you been working here?" I wondered aloud.

"About two months now. The state made me go to school in order to still get my benefits, so here I am."

"Do what you gotta' do." I told her. Then I said, "Is it still two police officers standing outside my door?"

It's only one now. I heard the other one went down to the cafeteria get something to eat. Why you ask?"

"No reason really."

"So, are you really under witness protection, like they say?" she began to probe while she took my blood pressure.

"If that's what you want to call it."

"Did they tell you how long you're supposed to be here?"

"Not yet. But I shouldn't be here too much longer."

The CNA chuckled. "You aren't from 'round here are you?"

"No, I'm not. But how did you guess?"

"You have a country accent."

"I'm from Virginia."

"What part?"

"Virginia Beach,"

"Really? Is Virginia Beach is as nice as everybody says it is?"

"Not to me, but I'm sure someone else would say differently." I commented while I watched her scribble something on my chart.

"Can you give me a number from one to ten describing your level of pain, ten being severe?"

"I'm like a six," I told her.

"Okay, well, I'm gonna give you another 5 mil. of codeine through your I.V." she told me.

"Okay, well, I'm gonna give you another 5 milliliters of morphine through your I.V." she told me. But when I looked I noticed that what she was about to shoot in my L.V. didn't look like it was hospital prescribed. The label on the bottle of clear liquid had in her hand looked old and part of it was scraped it off. The ink on the label was barely visible and that threw up a red flag for me. Something definitely wasn't right about this set up so I snatched my arm from her. "What are you doing? That shit you got in that bottle doesn't look like you got it from this hospital." I questioned her.

She tried to grab my arm back. "Give me your damn arm." She barked. And that's when I knew that this bitch was here to kill me. I also knew Bishop had to be behind it.

"Somebody help! She's trying to kill me!" I screamed. My voice cracked a few times because of my dry mouth. She tried to cover my mouth with one hand while she held onto the liquid filled syringe in the other. I tried to bite a plug out of her hand but she wouldn't let my teeth get close enough. I was recovering from a gunshot wound so I had hardly any energy left to fight this chick off me. I knew I had to react quickly or she'd defeat me so I reached down by my left thigh to press the nurse call button but she snatched it away from me.

"Shut up bitch and take it like a woman." She growled. Her face looked menacing. She was after blood and I was her target.

"Please help me! She's trying to kill me!" I screamed once more. This time my pitch was loud and it was clear. And in the blink of an eye one of the police officers standing guard outside my room burst into my room. I had never been so happy to see a man in uniform.

Once he realized what this chick was doing he pulled his pistol from his holster and pointed in our direction. "This is police, release the patient right now or I'm gonna shoot!" he boomed. His voice ricocheted off every wall in my room. It was like music to my heart. But his words didn't penetrate this woman at all. She was adamant about sticking me with whatever she had inside that syringe no matter who was around. I realized that immediately after she held the needle against my neck. The tip of the needle was pinching my neck. I figured if I moved one inch, I'd be in trouble. She was definitely on a mission. And that mission was to take me out.

"This is your last chance, release her right now or I'm gonna shoot." He boomed once more.

I had no idea who this woman was but I knew she had heart. It took balls to come into a hospital surrounded my cops to assassinate a government witness. She had to know that she'd be signing her death certificate if she got caught. But then I realized the affect Bishop had on women and chalked it up as the bitch being a total nut job. "Get back or I'll kill her!" she demanded after she jumped behind the head of my bed, using me as a shield.

I struggled with her because I was so weak. But when I saw the first chance I took it. Without giving it much thought I reached for the needle she had pressed against my neck and tried to snatch it from her hand. But this bitch wasn't willing to give up that easy. She tightened the grip around my neck and tried to choke me out. I started coughing hysterically.

INTERNATIONALLY KNOWN

"Please let me go," I begged as I tried to loosen the grip from around my neck.

"Now bitch, you're gonna die!" she threatened me once again.

At this point, I knew this chick wasn't going to let me go. It didn't matter to her that the police had just threatened to shoot her if she had not let me go. This chick had a death wish and before she went to glory, she decided she was going to take me with her.

While I struggled with trying to get her to loosen my neck I somehow started blanking out and then suddenly I started losing consciousness—, and then I heard a the police officer's gun fire. BOOM!

Stay Tuned

SNEAK PEEK AT

"GREEN EYE BANDIT"
IN STORES NOW

∎∎∎

PROLOGUE

My heart wouldn't accept what was going on around me. But my eyes knew better. Watching these monsters torture my sister Shelby had become unbearable. And every time I tried to look away, one of those goons snatched my head back by yanking my hair. "Nah bitch, you're gonna watch this." The guy roared and then he spit in my face.

My sister Shelby and I had always played a game or two of Russian roulette with our lives, but as fate would have it, our time had ran out. There was no way we were going to walk out of here alive. Even Shelby's probation officer Ms. Welch wasn't going to leave out of here breathing. Unfortunately, for her she planned an after hours home visit to our apartment so she could check on Shelby, and walked into a death trap. I knew she wished she had kept her field visits during business hours because now she's gotten herself into a bloody mess.

There were three guys surrounding us. They kicked in our front door and bum rushed our apartment

INTERNATIONALLY KNOWN

with their guns drawn and ready to fire. I knew why they were here so I tried to escape out of the apartment from our second story bathroom window, but Rocko quickly apprehended me and started the beating.

All three men looked menacing. They were average in height but they made up for their height in weight. They had to be at least two hundred pounds easy because the first time Shelby and I got hit in the face, it sounded like our jawbones cracked. Shelby screamed from the minute Rocko snatched her up by her neck until the time he hit her in her face. I saw the horror in her eyes and I saw our lives flash right before my eyes. It was going to be a sad night for the both of us. God help us all.

Breon and his henchmen came equipped with rope and duct tape, and tied us up to our kitchen chairs so we wouldn't have another chance to run. They even tied gags around our mouths to prevent us from letting the outside world know what was going on inside of our apartment. And it worked, because half way into the beating, Ms. Welch knocked on the front door. "Open the door Ms. Martin, it's me Ms. Welch." We all heard her say.

All three men looked at one another and then they looked at Shelby and I. The guy Breon wanted to know who was at the door. He pulled the duct tape from Shelby's mouth good enough for her to answer his questions. "It's my P.O. and she isn't going to leave until somebody opens the door," she warned him.

Breon motioned one of the guys to look through the peephole to see what Shelby's probation officer was doing on the other side of the door. The guy tiptoed to the front door and when he stepped on the loose wooden board directly in front of the door, it cracked and Ms. Welch heard it loud and clear. "Shelby, I hear you in there. Now if you don't open this door right now, I am going to have the police come and do it for me," she threatened, but no one moved. Breon waited for a moment to think and then a couple seconds later he instructed the guy at the door to open the door. "What if she wants to come in?" he objected.

"Just shut up and open it." Breon demanded in a low like whisper. But his pitch wasn't low enough because Ms. Welch heard him. "I hear you all talking in there. Now this will be the last time I tell you to open this door before I call the police for their assistance," she warned us.

The guy at the front door looked back at Breon once more. "Do it now." Breon instructed him once again. I could see that Breon was getting a little aggravated. The guy saw it too and decided to do as he was told. He turned back towards the front door and pulled the mask from his head. And not even a second later, he unlocked and opened the front door. The way our chairs were placed around the kitchen table, Shelby couldn't see the front door but I could.

Ms. Welch stood there before him and went into question mode that instant. "Where is Shelby?" she asked him.

"She's not here," the guy lied.

Ms. Welch sensed that he lied too, that's why she tried to look around him to get a good look into the apartment. The guy was too quick for her and moved to block her view. She didn't like that one bit. "Are you trying to hide something from me?" she questioned him once more.

"No, I'm not."

"What is your name young man?" her questions continued.

"My name is Antonio." He said flatly.

"Well Mr. Antonio, my name is Ms. Welch and I am Shelby's probation officer. And I am here today because she lied to me about sending in copies of her check stubs. Now, I'm going to need you to step aside so I can enter into this apartment."

"But I told you she's not here."

"I remember you saying that, but as her probation officer I have the right to search her dwelling at which time I see fit. And today would be one of those times," she tried to say it as politely as she could. Ms. Welch was one evil ass lady and when it came to home visits, she meant business. And the fact that this guy wasn't going to allow her to do what she wanted, she wasn't too happy about that.

While all of the commotion went on at the front door, Breon realized that his sidekick wasn't handling the situation with Shelby's probation officer as swiftly as he'd liked, so he stormed to the front door with his gun behind his back to see if he could make her go away. But what Breon failed to do was cover Shelby's mouth up before he walked off and left us in the kitchen.   And as soon as Breon turned the corner, Shelby screamed as loud as she could and said, "Ms. Welch run and call the police."

Breon turned back around and rushed towards Shelby.   When he got within arms reach of her, he lunged back and punched her in the face as hard as he could. The force behind his punch knocked Shelby backwards onto the floor.   And when I thought I'd seen enough, he started kicking her in her side while her arms were tied behind her back and her ankles tied to the legs of the chair.   She looked so helpless on the floor and I couldn't do a thing to help her.   She cried her poor heart out while Breon kicked and stomped her with his fucking Timberland boots.   I swear if I had the strength to break loose from these restraints, I'd have his fucking head on a chopping block, digging his eyes out of his fucking head.

While Breon was beating the shit out of my sister, the other guy had no choice but to grab Ms. Welch and drag her into the apartment.   She put up a big fight to get away from him but when Breon's other henchman saw that his partner needed help in getting Ms. Welch under control, he went to his aid.   With both men attacking her at the same time, Ms. Welch didn't have a fighting chance.   And after she suffered consistent blows to her body and head, she lost consciousness.

"Breon, we gon' need some help picking her big ass up from the floor.   I heard one guy say.

"One of y'all help me pick this bitch up from the floor first." Breon demanded. He had stopped hitting and kicking Shelby by this time. So, after Breon and one of the other guys helped sit Shelby's chair back on it's feet, all three of them managed to pick Ms. Welch up and sat her in a chair next to us. They didn't waste any time bounding and gagging her.

I could tell that she was clinging onto life. And right before the beating started, she begged those fucking monsters to spare her. "I'm not the one you want." She pleaded. But they ignored her cries and proceeded to beat her across her face. I literally cried for her and Shelby, because I felt their pain and I knew that my time was coming next.

Breon's heartless ass washed Shelby's blood from his arms and hands. He dried them off by wiping his palms directly across the thigh part of his jeans. I watched him very closely through my glassy eyes. I was furious about everything I had witnessed and I wanted my revenge. But that feat looked impossible from where I was sitting, so I sat quickly and prayed a silent prayer.

"Don't close those green eyes now bitch! 'Cause your ass is next." Breon warned me and then I heard his footsteps coming in my direction. I stopped midway in my prayer and opened my eyes. I tried to scream when I saw that he had his gun pointed directly at Shelby, but I was unable to do so with the duct tape wrapped tightly around my mouth. Tears started falling rapidly. And my heart began to beat erratically.

KIKI SWINSON

She was done and I knew it. So, I took one last look at her and watched Breon pull the trigger. BOOM!

INTERNATIONALLY KNOWN

GREEN EYE BANDIT/ THE COME UP

The temperature throughout the hotel suite was set at 70 degrees, but sweat pellets emerged from the pores of my forehead and underneath my armpits like I was sitting inside of a fucking sauna. I swear I couldn't get out of this place quick enough. I had just taken a bunch of cash from a black, Marc Jacobs handcrafted leather wallet that belonged to this guy my sister Shelby was fucking in the next room. When I first arrived in the hotel room, I heard Shelby moaning like her mind was going bad. It sounded like she was getting her pussy ate and when I peeped in on the action, my suspicions were confirmed. That cracker she had feasting between her legs was putting in overtime. I almost got up the nerve to ask him to give me some of his tongue action. But after I snapped back into reality about what I came there to do, I decided against it.

A few minutes after I started going through the man's things, I realized he and Shelby had switched positions. "Damn girl, you sure know how to suck the meat off my dick!" I heard him say to Shelby.

"I make you........feel........good, huh?" Shelby replied between licks.

I laughed of course because Shelby was a class act. She was a master at making guys weak at their knees. Shelby was a sexy, 135lbs., bombshell. She was a very pretty young woman with a body to die for.

KIKI SWINSON

Her caramel complexion, long, straight, dark brown hair, and her big hazel colored eyes were the perfect combination. It wasn't hard to tell that she was half Cuban and black. From the time we were young girls, boys would always throw themselves at her. And while she had them literally eating out of her hands, she could never keep a man around long enough to have a solid relationship, so she did the next best thing; trick with them. She gave them what they wanted and in return they gave her what she wanted. It was a win-win situation in her eyes.

The joker she had in her grasp tonight was a white investment banker from Maryland in town for a conference. According to the driver's license in his wallet, his name was Alex Leman. He was born in 1962, he resided in the city of Baltimore, and he was an organ donor. How freaking patriotic of him? The old dude had a soft spot for humanity. Sorry to say he had a kinky side to him as well. And since tonight was his last night in town, Shelby and I seized this opportunity to come up on some major dough. I got him for every crisp one hundred dollar bill he had tucked away in his wallet. I hadn't had a chance to count them, but there had to be at least twelve of them in all. He also had a few major credit cards like an American Express and Discover card, but I left them alone. I wasn't about to get caught on camera in some department store trying to buy a bunch of bullshit with stolen credit cards. I wanted my money free and clear. Too bad, I can't say the same about Shelby. She'd snatch this guy's credit cards up in a heartbeat. It didn't matter to her that she was on probation, because she had already been charged and convicted of credit card fraud a year ago. But I cared and as long as she turned the tricks and I did the taking, I vowed to do things my way.

Immediately after I had taken all of the money this guy Alex had, I stuffed it inside of my pants pocket and headed towards the door of the hotel suite. But before I could sneak back out of the hotel room, some asshole knocked on the fucking door. I panicked and almost pissed in my pants. How in the hell could someone come at a time like this? I rushed to the door and looked through the peephole. To my surprise, my co-worker Mitch from room service was standing on the other side of the door with a bottle of champagne in a bucket of ice and two champagne glasses placed on a rolling table. My first reaction was to open the door and tell Mitch to carry his ass, but then I realized how he'd react seeing me in this room, so I decided against it. Two seconds later, Mitch knocked on the door again and then he yelled out the words, "Room service."

I literally almost passed out right there in the hallway. But when I heard Alex scramble to his feet to get the door, I jumped into the hallway closet and slid the door closed. "I'm coming," I heard Shelby's sex partner yell as soon as he got within several feet of the door to his suite.

I couldn't see Alex as he made his way to the door, but I heard every move he made from the time he opened the door to let Mitch roll the table inside the room until he started questioning Shelby, who had followed him to the door. "Wait a minute," he said and then he fell silent.

"What's the matter?" Shelby questioned him.

"I had over fifteen hundred dollars in my fucking wallet and now it's gone." he said.

"Are you sure?" Shelby asked.

"You goddamn right I'm sure!" he roared.

"Why are you snapping at me?" I heard Shelby say.

"Because my money is gone and you've been the only one in this room."

"So, you're accusing me of taking your fucking money? she snapped back.

"Who else could've taken it?" Alex stood his ground.

"First of all, I've been by your side the entire time I've been in this fucking room. So, how in the hell could I have taken the money?" Shelby reasoned.

Before Alex responded to Shelby, Mitch interjected, "Sir, don't worry about it. Just call room service and have them charge the champagne and the strawberries to your room." Then I heard the door close.

Seconds later, I heard Shelby say, "I can't believe you just accused me of stealing your fucking money."

But Alex didn't respond to her. He remained completely quiet. They continued to stand outside of the closet door, so I was literally in the center of all the action. I just wished that I could see what they were doing.

"Why the fuck are you just standing there and looking at me like you're insane?" Shelby continued.

So again, I waited to hear Alex's response. And to my surprise, he didn't utter one word. I did however hear sudden movement and then I heard a loud boom sound. "What the fuck are you doing? Get off of me." Shelby said, her voice was barely audible.

"I going to kill you, you black bitch!" he grinded his teeth. "You're gonna wish you never laid eyes on me." He continued.

Then I heard Shelby coughing. "Get off me!" She managed to say.

My heart raced as I listened to the commotion outside of the closet door. It was apparent that Alex was choking Shelby to her death. And that's when it popped in my head that if I didn't stop him, I'd have one dead sister. So, within seconds, I burst out of the closet door and was able to witness first hand how badly Alex was hurting her.

Right after I burst onto the scene, I noticed how shocked they both were to see me. "Get the fuck off of her!" I demanded as I stormed towards his 5'10 frame. He looked like he weighed 150lbs., but that didn't at all intimidate me, even though I was at least 30lbs., lighter. I used to run track back when I was in high school, so I was physically fit.

"What the fuck?" Alex uttered from his lips. He was definitely at a lost for words when he realized that he and Shelby weren't alone. And while he had Shelby's back against the wall, he had both of his hands around her neck, leaving himself vulnerable for me to intervene. This guy was on a mission to choke the life out of her. So I lunged towards the back of his head with my fist and clocked him as hard as I could. I followed that blow with several more punches, and then I threw my right arm around his neck and grabbed him into a chokehold. "Let her go." I demanded as I applied pressure to his neck.

He struggled to keep Shelby within his grasp and when he realized that I wasn't going to let him go, he started loosening the grip around her neck and then he finally let her go. "Alright. I let her go. Now you let me go," he pleaded.

"If I let you go, you ain't gonna try no funny shit, right?" I questioned him.

"No. I swear I won't." he assured me. But I wasn't feeling his answer. Something told me that this guy couldn't be trusted. He had already tried to murk Shelby, so why wouldn't he try to throw shade on both of us in this damn hotel room? If he really wanted to fuck us over, he could call the cops on our asses and get me and Shelby locked up for trespassing and robbery and that would not have been a good look on our part.

"How do I know if you'll try some dumb shit?" I asked him.

"Look, lady I don't want any problems. Just take your friend and leave and I'll forget that any of this happened." He managed to say while I continued to hold him in the chokehold.

I looked at Shelby who was only three feet away from me. I searched her face for any sign about which course of action we should take. And when she instructed me to keep him hemmed up until she gathered up her things, I did just that. "A'ight. But hurry up." I yelled aloud as she disappeared into the other room.

Meanwhile Alex became a little antsy while I had him in the chokehold. "You do know that I could have both of you bitches arrested" he commented.

I tightened the grip around his neck just a bit more. "Shut the hell up before I call your wife and tell her how you like eating black pussy." I said.

After I threatened to spill the beans on his ass, he immediately changed his tune. "Look, just get out of my hotel room and take your friend with you," he said.

Moments later, Shelby showed back up fully dressed with her handbag clutched tightly in her right hand. "Come on, let's go." she yelled and then she rushed towards the door........,

Stay Tuned